# TREACHERY ON THE HIGH SEAS

A man hurled himself at Capt'n Errol who met the charge head-on with swinging fists. Flesh crashing against flesh, both men went down, rolling along the deck, pummeling each other savagely. Ki lifted an assailant bodily, juggled him in his arms, and hurled him far out into the harbor, where he hit with a splash. Jessie laid waste with a hardwood rope pin. Curses, howls, and the wicked impact of clubs crashing against flesh-and-bone targets.

In a solid fighting line the crew stood shoulder to shoulder against the Vermillion hirelings, driving them back, inch by inch, until only the rail and the water lay between them.

Then one of the men flashed a gun. Ki swore savagely, as gunfire slashed through the night. Pistols blazed from the decks, then there was nothing but the sound of the engines, the song of the escaping steam, and the increasing hiss of the bow wave as the *Snohomish* throbbed to life, swinging her nose out into the harbor toward Puget Sound . . .

\*   \*   \*

This title includes an exciting excerpt from *Sixkiller* by Giles Tippette, available from Jove Books in May 1992!

The Paperback Trade
843-2947

→• WESLEY ELLIS •←

# LONE STAR

## AND THE
## DEEP WATER PIRATES

JOVE BOOKS, NEW YORK

LONE STAR AND THE DEEPWATER PIRATES

A Jove Book / published by arrangement with
the author

PRINTING HISTORY
Jove edition / April 1992

ISBN: 0-515-10833-2

Jove Books are published by The Berkley Publishing Group,
200 Madison Avenue, New York, New York 10016.
The name "JOVE" and the "J" logo
are trademarks belonging to Jove Publications, Inc.

PRINTED IN THE UNITED STATES OF AMERICA

10  9  8  7  6  5  4  3  2  1

# Chapter 1

Seafarin' troubles come in trios, like Neptune's trident. Jessica Starbuck was reminded of that old sailor's bromide as she stood at the bridge rail of the *Snohomish*, watching the deckhands and salmon cannery crew file slowly aboard.

The *Snohomish* was an elderly single-stack coastal steamer, its curving wooden sides scarred by wind and rain and sun, its splintered deckhouse and rails gouged by bullets and knives and arrows. On either side the Seattle Harbor slips were lined with other steamers, smaller packets, tugs, and tall-poled fish trollers. Dockside, a swarm of toiling roustabouts moved past one another, ignoring the chilly spring rain, trundling scores of barrels, crates, and cases to and from warehouses and freight decks.

On the aft deck Jessie noticed Ki, her long-time companion, standing out of the rain under a canvas awning, looking over the arriving crewmen. They, too, saw his attention and met it with a solid, unyielding scrutiny.

1

Next to Jessie the ship's captain, Genovese Belluche, took his old briar pipe out of his mouth and remarked, "They're sure sizing you two up, Miz Starbuck. Before he got laid low, ol' Moses Laird was a holy terror handling cattle rustlers on the range and fish pirates in the north, and his son Errol was a chip off the same block, up till the lawdogs sent him to prison. But they don't know about you."

"You can fairly feel their doubt in the air," Jessie admitted. "Is it my imagination, or are there a lot of new faces among your crew?"

"Aye, I've had to hire replacements." Belluche frowned, not liking what he had to say. "Picked 'em up in a waterfront bar," he muttered. "Half the reg'ar crew deserted."

"Deserted? Why?"

"Well, now, ma'am . . ." Belluche trailed off, embarrassed, then hastily continued: "When they didn't show up, I made a round of the bars. Found some of 'em full of rotgut and not fit for work. Those that could talk said they were through."

Jessie's golden-green eyes grew dark and troubled as she scanned the men coming over the side. Each weather-seamed face lifted briefly, and she was increasingly conscious of their unsure, even suspicious expressions. Theirs was no idle curiosity. This was the first time in nearly twenty years that Ol' Boss, Moses Laird, and his son, Capt'n Errol, wouldn't be taking crews north to pack salmon.

Rumor traveled fast along waterfronts. Everyone knew Ol' Boss was lying at death's door in the hospital, and that Capt'n Errol was serving a sentence for dereliction of duty after the sinking of *Snohomish*'s sister ship, the *Hecate*. Some said it'd been the sinking that sickened Ol' Boss unto death; Ol' Boss denied it. But it was unquestionably true that, following the *Hecate*'s loss, he'd been forced to borrow heavily to operate his remaining ship and keep his business, the Oceana Fish Company, afloat through this season. Everything the Lairds owned, everything they had worked for all their lives, was riding on the success of the upcoming salmon catch. Now ugly stories were being passed around about the *Snohomish*. And many of the experienced hands were deserting, and their replacements were as scummy a lot as Jessie had ever seen.

And yet, much as it rankled her, she couldn't blame them too much. After all, she was taking the crew to the Glacier Inlet cannery this year—she, an untested young *female*, for chrissakes! But it went beyond a sailor's natural reluctance to take orders from a woman.

In lean years, Jessie knew, the Ol' Boss had taken care of his men somehow and had promised pensions when they were too old to work. Already his pension list was a heavy financial drain in these days of sharp competition. Aside from her being a woman, the old hands were afraid she might have different ideas. She might cut expenses to the bone; might lay off those whose strength and agility had slowed down, in a calling that exacts speed.

Those who were newly hired on were nonetheless experienced. They knew that a coastwise trip to can salmon was considered anything but a lush berth. It meant a season of cramped quarters, skimpy food, and monotony—if the weather was good. If they ran into an Arctic blow, it mean wet, frigid misery. A cannery-tender didn't have a chance of riding the seas like an ordinary vessel. Its only choice was to try to club the combers down to size. It was usually touch and go as to which would win, but in any case the crew was always the loser. All in all a man had to be pretty broke, or drunk, to ship on a coastwise tender. Jessie had a hunch that this bunch of replacements was probably both.

If that weren't enough, what with Ol' Boss and Capt'n Errol both gone, this season chances were great that the fish pirates—those two-legged wolves infesting coastal waters from the Columbia River to the Bering Sea—would be sure to raid Oceana Fish Company's traps. If they stopped the flow of salmon to the cannery, then a business Moses Laird had spent a lifetime in building would crash. Those who bought the salvage wouldn't be interested in paying pensions or keeping on rummy replacements.

And so the crewmen studied Jessie and Ki as they plodded up the gangplank, backs bent under the weight of tightly packed duffel bags and suitcases. Old hands and replacements alike searched for flaws and weakness of character, probing for signs that might indicate lack of decision or courage in a critical situation. Their lives, as well as livelihood, damned well depended on it.

What they saw in Jessie was a tall, lissome woman in her twenties, wearing an oilskin slicker whose yellowish color nearly matched her long coppery-blonde hair, which she had tucked up under the crown of her brown Stetson. And though the slicker was buttoned at the neck and completely covered her silk blouse, jeans, and denim jacket, it failed to hide the firm thrust of her breasts or the sensual curves of her thighs and buttocks. Nor did the nippy weather chill the sultry warmth of her suntanned face with its high cheekbones, audacious eyes, and the provocative if sometimes humorous lilt of her lips.

However, her features couldn't help mirroring the exhaustive effects of her long journey. It seemed forever since she had left her Circle Star Ranch in Texas on a business trip through lower California. Then this situation cropped up, and instead of returning home as planned, she boarded a coastal packet for a ten-day voyage up the coast to Seattle. She felt drained by it all, and yet, at the moment

4

she also reflected her grave determination to meet and beat this latest threat. That was why she carried her custom .38 Colt pistol in a holstered gunbelt around her waist, and a two-shot derringer tucked behind the wide buckle of her belt. A lady could never be too careful.

Unlike Jessie, Ki showed no sign of emotion one way or another. He was tired of the boring confinement of shipboard life, though, being a man whose lean, sinewy body was graced with energy and stamina. He, too, was swathed in a slicker, his hatbrim tugged low and visoring features that appealed to women who liked their lovers tempered by experience. Born of a Japanese woman wedded to an American, he was a handsome blend of both races—tall, bronze-completed, with blue-black straight hair, a strong-boned face, and almond eyes of a dark and vital intensity. Orphaned in Japan, he had emigrated to America, where he had been hired by Jessie's father, Alex Starbuck, a wealthy international magnate. When, ultimately, Alex Starbuck was murdered, Ki became the confidant of Starbuck's only child, Jessica, whom by then Ki had known for so long that they were as close as blood brother and sister; now, in his early thirties, he was ready as ever to protect Jessie and her far-flung interests.

As befitting his role, Ki wore nondescript jeans, a collarless shirt, an old leather vest, and, instead of boots, a pair of rope-soled cloth slippers. He didn't pack a gun, nor did he use one as a rule. Yet he was anything but defenseless. Lethal power lay in his relaxed yet iron-hard body, for he was a samurai—trained in the martial arts, an expert with the slim daggers and other weapons, including little star-shaped razored disks called *shuriken*, which were stashed in his vest.

Captain Belluche, hired by Ol' Boss Laird to skipper the *Snohomish*, snapped his teeth together with an audible click. "Don't like this, none of this. Oceana Fish ain't never been cursed with such troubles afore. Something behind it all, I swear." Still giving the new hands a stiff scrutiny, and accompanied by Jessie, he descended to the aft deck and joined Ki under the awning. "Keep watch on these new men, Ki. If any of 'em act funny, let me know."

Ki nodded taciturnly. Looking them over, he searched for any interesting details of appearance that would imprint them individually in his mind. Like a broken nose, for instance. There was one. A bandy-legged man with top-heavy shoulders and coarse black hair was wearing a broad strip of adhesive tape across the bridge of his nose.

"Looks like someone busted you on the beak," Ki said conversationally.

The man sneered. "Caught it in a swinging door, Slant-eyes. Is this tub hiring sailors, or running a body beautiful contest?"

"Sailors," Belluche responded gruffly, "but ones who can keep their tongues behind their teeth."

The man's jaw pushed forward, but he moved on without a word.

Captain Belluche greeted the returning hands and the new men he knew personally, and named them off as they passed Jessie and Ki. Among them was Gimper Tynes, with his wooden peg and direct, glittering eyes. Dour Duncan McArdle, who'd lost his first-mate's license due to drunkenness. Hawser Yocum, ace of the McKenzie River in times gone by. Pierre Quinotte, who had swept keel boats down to St. Louis in the golden days of fur. And huge-handed, towering Chinook Norris, the ship's engineer and boilerman. They and the others were for the most part men of poor reputations, questionable loyalties,

6

or vicious habits—or all three—many banned from working for the bigger, high-toned steamship lines, some bound to the land by ties of bitterness or booze, few with good cause to like Oceana Fish or the *Snohomish*.

Belluche knew hardly any of the cannery crew, the majority of whom were Filipino or Chinese, dressed in black smocks, cheap rubber-soled shoes, and no socks. To Ki, however, as each yellow face lifted briefly to scan them, he was increasingly conscious of their penetrating eyes—Oriental eyes, mysterious, inscrutable, keenly appraising. Then he noticed Belluche stiffen as a pasty-faced man came up the gangplank.

"Jack Wing," Belluche growled. "Half white, half Chinese. With none of the good points and all of the bad of both races. He's Fantan Monger's gamblin' partner. Monger'll be along. Look, there he is now, tryin' to hide his face behind that fat-bellied mucker beside him."

Ki looked at Jack Wing and thought of a knife thrust in the darkness, but the powerfully built Monger suggested a bludgeon or dynamite until he glanced at the man's hands. They were big, but there was a swiftness and grace of a woman's about them. They were hands made for the manipulation of cards.

"When the steamer heads south, gamblers like Wing and Monger magically appear and start their crooked games," Belluche continued. "By the time the *Snohomish* docks in Seattle, them sharks have taken the major portion of the season's payroll. Worse yet, scuttlebutt has it that there's a tie-up between Monger and Boone Vermillion."

Jessie and Ki exchanged glances. A couple of days ago, when they'd first arrived in Seattle and visited Moses Laird in the hospital, Laird had warned them of Vermillion. A rival operator without any scruples, the man had ruined several canneries by robbing their traps. A successful fish pirate must be skilled in the finer points of bribery and murder in dealing with the trap guards, and according to Laird, Vermillion was one of the best. It made Jessie and Ki wonder if Vermillion might not be readying to pounce on problem-plagued Oceana Fish, or even to have been scheming from the first to cripple the company.

Jessie remarked to Belluche, "A link between Vermillion and that pair has possibilities, all right. If Monger and Wing work on the crew and Vermillion on the fish trap, there won't be anything left of Oceana this fall."

"I'm going over and tell 'em they're not wanted," Belluche said. "Might as well get the jump on trouble they'll dish up."

"In that case, I might as well start keeping them off your back," Ki said, following the captain.

A hush suddenly settled across the deck as Ki and Belluche approached. With no exchange of words there was mass agreement that the new bosses were facing their first test.

Belluche clamped a hand on Monger's arm, stopping him. Jack Wing pulled up short, and so did the "fat-bellied mucker"—evidently there were three to contend with, and the unnamed man was a whiskery brute almost large enough to count as two.

"Turn y'self and your gear around, Monger, and git ashore," Belluche ordered. "Take Jack Wing with you."

"Why?" Monger asked insolently.

"You know why," Belluche retorted. "It's none of Miz Starbuck's business what these boys do with their money after they get back to Seattle. But I'm going to see to it for her that you two don't clean them while they're aboard."

Monger scowled; Wing's face set in stubborn lines. The take was so great they could afford to go north with a cannery crew, labor with the men during the salmon run, then make the return trip. Female relatives were usually on hand when a ship docked, often for the expressed purpose of circumventing gamblers. They not only took charge of their men but the season's pay as well. Aboard ship it was different. Gambling was infectious. The best resolutions went overboard when there was mass excitement and the stakes were high.

"Get going!" Belluche stood tall—or as tall as his short, stout frame would allow. Other than Ki there was nobody to keep people off his back should trouble erupt, but he acted indifferent to his jeopardy. "I said, get going, Monger!"

Wing spoke up. "Better think it over," he warned, clearly as disinclined to move as Monger. To have done so would have involved loss of face, and face was of tremendous importance in Oriental eyes. And referring to that, he added menacingly, "Otherwise the bitch'll lose face in more ways than one."

Belluche put pressure on Monger's arm to turn him.

"Leggo!" Monger wrenched free of Belluche's grip as though it were a snake biting his arm, then pivoted and punched the captain in the right eye. "I'll learn you to butt in," he snarled and mashed Belluche's face against a steel support beam with a dull, meaty crunch. Dazed and blinded, Belluche reeled to one side and began falling to the deck, and Monger drew back his right foot to kick his boot into Belluche's unprotected belly. "I'll learn you good, you ol' fart!"

Ki reacted before the kick could land. With an odd smile that masked his anger, he launched himself at Monger, who immediately turned to meet him with clenched fists. Ki ducked Monger's first and last punch, catching the gambler's outflung arm and angling to drop to

9

one knee, swinging him into *seoi otoshi*, the kneeling shoulder-throw.

Monger arched through the air, over the heads of the onlookers, and came down on the fantail. He sprawled there, dazed and breathless.

Even before Monger hit, Ki was swinging around on the rain-slickened deck, to check whatever Wing and the other man might be up to. The other man, who was nearer, was charging him with outstretched arms, as if he were tackling a drunk in a barroom brawl. Ki chopped the edge of his hand down at the man's nose. He purposely held back a little so he would not smash it flat, but it struck forcefully enough to hurt like hell, and tears of pain sprang into the man's eyes. Ki followed through by kicking the man in the side of his knee, collapsing him to one side. He caught his right arm, crunched down on it with his elbow, and then brought his own knee into his hip.

The man dropped to the deck, leaving the way clear for Wing to lash out at Ki with his wide leather belt. Ki had already seen Wing slide off his belt and fold it double, which was one of the reasons he'd dumped the other man as he had, for now he was able to step over the man and catch hold of Wing's right arm and left shoulder with his hands. At the same time Ki moved his right foot slightly in back of Wing so that as Wing began tumbling sideward, Ki was able to dip to his right knee and yank viciously. His *hizi otoshi*, or elbow-drop, worded perfectly; Wing catapulted upside-down and collapsed jarringly on top of the other man, flattening them both to the deck.

And Monger, face purpling with rage, launched himself off the fantail, a well-honed gutting knife clutched in his right hand. "I'm gonna carve you apart!" he bellowed, slashing at Ki.

10

Ki calmly stepped aside and then kicked up with his calloused foot. His heel caught Monger smack on his chin, so hard that Monger flew backward, sliding on the slippery deckplates, caromed against the railing, and tipped overboard. There was a short, rapidly diminishing wail, followed by a loud splash and a gusher of brackish harbor water.

The encircling crowd of deckhands and cannery crew gaped at the spot where Monger went over, his two moaning pals, and then at Ki with stunned disbelief. They said nothing.

Jessie broke the silence. "Some of you, get these bums and their gear off this boat, pronto!"

"My pleasure," Belluche growled through bloody lips. Fairly recovered now, he hauled Wing up and began kicking him toward the gangplank. Ki followed with the other man, and behind came several Filipinos carrying the belongings of Monger and the beaten pair.

Dockside, Monger could be spotted nearby, struggling to climb out of the water. Between gasping breaths, he was swearing luridly.

Belluche grunted with satisfaction. "Well, I'm going back aboard and wash up," he told Ki.

Ki nodded. "Sure," he said, "and a little raw beefsteak will go well on your right eye, Capt'n."

★

# Chapter 2

Visiting hours at King County Hospital were about over when Jessie, accompanied by Captain Belluche, left the *Snohomish* to go see Ol' Boss, Moses Laird. By then things had calmed down, and all the crew was aboard, with the first mate and Ki in charge. But time and washing hadn't reduced the swelling of Belluche's lips and right eye very much.

Darting in front of a laboring team of bays hauling a loaded freight wagon, Jessie and the captain swung left along the wide dock and moved swiftly past a string of two- and three-storied warehouses. They picked their way around scattered boxes and crates, while bearded stevedores, toiling at ropes and pulleys, hauled barrels of flour and other staples in great rope slings up to storage platforms.

An abrupt shrill shout of warning beside Jessie turned her half around. Then she was propelled sideward by the thrust of hands smacking her shoulder. Off-balance, her head craned instinctively upward. She had a fleeting, horrible glimpse of three barrels far above her.

One moment they were being drawn into space, firmly encompassed by the stout rope sling around their sides. Then there was a snapping sound. The barrels hurtled toward her.

She was already falling sideways. She hit the dock and rolled frantically. A man screamed, his cry suddenly silenced as the dock shook to a tremendous, splintering impact. A white shower of flour boiled into the air. The wind carried it across the waterfront in a drifting cloud, great mounds of it fluttering down upon Jessie. She struggled up through that choking veil, gasping for breath. And all the while she heard the agonizing moans of Captain Belluche, who was trapped beneath the plummeting barrels.

Jessie wiped a sleeve across her face and eyes. She beat at the flour that clung to her clothes. Men were yelling and shouting, moving toward her and the smashed remains of the flour barrels, under which was the prone, writhing shape of the captain, who had saved Jessie while allowing himself to be trapped under their falling weight.

"Captain! Captain Belluche!" Jessie gasped, kneeling alongside.

"M'legs," Belluche groaned weakly. Color had drained from his face, and his tobacco-stained teeth were on edge as he fought to hold on to consciousness. "My innards, too . . ."

There was blood under Belluche's side. It made a sticky, scarlet pool in the flour and kept widening. His legs had a crushed, beaten look.

"S-saw that rope bust, knew you . . . you'd be right under it—" He broke off. His lips trembled and his eyes fluttered, then closed. Sailors, roustabouts, and laborers were crowding up close. Jessie rose from her crouch, her

14

face hard and hot as she lashed out at them.

"Don't stand there and gape like fools! Lend me a hand, someone! We've got to get Captain Belluche to the hospital!"

For just a brief instant the crowd was immobile. In that interval Jessie's eyes glanced upward to the loading platform of the warehouse, and she glimpsed a dark, watching figure suddenly wheel and disappear into the shadows. Her eyes narrowed then, passing along the stump of the rope dangling in space, and the skin pulled so tightly over her cheekbones that her expression looked distinctly gaunt. Then she bent down, got a firm yet tender grip under Belluche's armpits. She alone did not have the strength to pull him free, but her action triggered a response in the bystanders, and several men took hold of the captain, easing him from under the wreckage, while a dozen eager roustabouts cleared a path through the crowd.

Jessie began following, then cut across to the warehouse. The building, like the two on either side of it, carried the name of Boone Vermillion as owner. Into the dockside entrance she turned, shoulders moving restlessly, hands balled into unladylike fists.

In the uncertain gloom of the musty warehouse she collided with a man. The man cursed and lunged away. But Jessie stopped him, spinning him around with a hard grip on his arm.

"What's your rush?" she demanded.

He had a rough, swarthy face, and his dark, close-spaced eyes glared malevolently at her. "Git your hands off'n me, sister!"

"If I'm not mistaken, you were up on the loading platform of this warehouse a few minutes ago when that rope sling broke."

15

"Not me." The man brushed Jessie's arm away and stood wide-legged and defiant. "I was nowhere near that sling."

They were close to the door of the warehouse. A few curious men had tagged after Jessie, and now a bearded roustabout pushed in from the dock. "You're lyin', Hank Pierce," the roustabout declared. "I was dockside when it happened. Believe me, ma'am, this-here Pierce and another gent were handlin' the sling."

Hank Pierce pivoted to face the roustabout, his cheeks reddening. "Keep your nose outta my business, frien', if'n you don't want a bellyful of lead," he growled and stabbed at the Navy Colt at his waist.

But Jessie moved in quickly, her own revolver snaking out of the holster in a lightning blur of speed. The muzzle jabbed Pierce's middle. "It's your belly that'll get the lead if you don't let loose of your gun."

Paling, Pierce glanced around at the bystanders. "Jezus, you guys, grab her! No female pistol-packer's any lady or a shootist!"

"That's what we's afeared of," one of the men replied, none too sympathetically. "She might go wavery and hit us by mistake, if she takes notion to fire point-blank at you."

"F'Gawd's sake!"

"You admit you were up on that loading platform?" Jessie persisted.

"What if I was up there?" Pierce retorted, his bravado belied by a quaver in his voice. "I'm the manager of this warehouse, after all. Besides, that was purely an accident when the sling busted."

"I'm not sure it was an accident," Jessie snapped. There was cold savagery in her tone. "For two reasons. Because you were working the sling, and because this place belongs

16

to Boone Vermillion." She jabbed the gun muzzle harshly into Pierce's gut. "We'll have a look upstairs just to be sure. March!"

Fury put a shining gray brilliance in Pierce's eyes, but he was helpless under the threat of Jessie's gun. Finally he turned and tramped to a stairway along the side of the building. Jessie and the onlookers followed. They reached the upper story and threaded their way around the litter of barrels and crates that were strewn about the floor. While the bystanders watched Pierce, Jessie strode to the swinging end of rope that hung from the pulley wheel. She frowned when she saw that the break was uneven.

Seeing the frown, Pierce laughed tauntingly. "Well, sister, what'd you find, eh? You were reckonin' somebody cut the rope with a knife, and now you see you was wrong."

Jessie spun about, her eyes riveted upon the warehouse foreman. "Maybe you were just smarter than you look," she said. "You could've slashed or hacked the rope unevenly, leaving it weakened so it would break under strain when you were ready."

"You've got a helluva lot of gall sayin' that," Pierce snarled. "I'll see Vermillion hears about this."

"Don't worry. I've a feeling I'll be telling him myself." Jessie came up to Pierce. "From now on I'll be watching you, Hank Pierce. I've got no proof—yet—but I still think you had orders to kill me and Captain Belluche. Don't give me another excuse to kill you!"

After leaving the warehouse, Jessie went on along the wharf and started up the hill in the direction of the hospital. Seattle was alive with a moving tide of people. She listened to the cacophony of the waterfront and the raucous tinkle of the honky-tonks, the creak of laden freight wagons and the bawdy shouts of leather-lunged teamsters . . . and she

17

wondered what she was going to do, now that Captain Belluche was grievously crippled, if not outright dead.

Perhaps, she hoped, Belluche could recommend another captain to take his place at the last minute. If not, she'd have to ask Moses Laird, and she dreaded the thought of relating this latest disaster to the Ol' Boss. He was in no condition to take the blow—if he were, he never would've signed over his company to Starbuck to run; he would've been up fighting, as he always had before.

It had come as a complete surprise to Jessie when Moses Laird turned Oceana Fish over to Starbuck the month before. It was his right, of course, for Starbuck was an investment partner in Oceana for almost two decades, dating back to when Jessie's father, Alex Starbuck, had been expanding his Pacific Coast ventures. Alex Starbuck and Moses Laird had taken to each other, worked together, and Laird had even given refuge to Starbuck at great personal risk, without question or compensation, saving him from enemies who were hunting him down. Then, after Alex Starbuck had been murdered, Jessie had heard little from Moses Laird—other than a brief note saying his wife had sickened and died—until his telegram relinquishing control had arrived, without warning or explanation, at Starbuck headquarters on her Circle Star Ranch. That had been alarming, for the Ol' Boss had pulled his family fortunes through many a storm.

Immediately Jessie had requested information from her Starbuck field operatives in the Seattle region. Swiftly they had reported back the news of Laird's hospitalization and his son's imprisonment. Both the salmon cannery in Alaska and the logging camp on Puget Sound were in critical condition financially, and suspicions were that Boone Vermillion was readying to move in for the kill. Boone Vermillion was a name Jessie knew; he'd been a thorn in Starbuck's side in other business dealings. Even the hint that Vermillion was involved convinced her that Laird's problems were serious—meaning dangerous—but that didn't matter. Alex Starbuck never forgot a debt or a friend; neither did Jessie. Ol' Man Moses Laird hadn't asked for help, exactly, but he was going to get it. With interest.

Now, as she glanced up at the dark stone facade of the hospital, Jessie vowed her commitment to see this through. Entering the ground-floor clinic which served as an emergency room, she saw Captain Belluche lying unconscious on the simple operating table, bloodied trousers cut open, and a doctor grimly treating his mangled legs.

"He's in bad shape," the doctor said in answer to Jessie's question. "Compound fractures of both legs, along with some crushment of bone, I'm afraid, and tearing of the nerve tissues."

"Do what you can," Jessie urged; her voice was oddly soft, yet all the more dominant and penetrating. "I want you to bring him through. Charge everything to me. I'll be back."

Jessie whirled out of the clinic, leaving the medico staring after her in open-mouthed astonishment. Other men who had stepped up to the door backed away as she strode through, on into the hospital proper. Locating Ol' Boss Laird's room, she saw the usual "No Visitors" card on the door. As she was opening the door, an orderly rushed over, trying to stop her.

"He's pretty low," the orderly cautioned. "You can't—"

"Can't help it," Jessie replied brusquely and entered.

Gray shadows lay heavily within the curtained room, shrouding the bed and Moses Laird's wasted body. It seemed to her the darkness was an omen. Gently she said, "How're you feeling, Ol' Boss?"

The big, white-haired man with the bony shoulders and pain-etched face stirred and opened his eyes. "Jessie . . ." he whispered and managed to grin, gesturing feebly. "Jessie, meet my cub."

From out of the murky far corner appeared another figure, that of a tall, rangy man, and to her shock Jessie realized that it was indeed Errol Laird. Lean and sinewy and hard, with narrow hips and wide shoulders, somber in worn seaman's blues and cloth cap, Capt'n Errol acknowledged Jessie with a nod and a quick wave of his hand. It was a thick, strong, scarred hand.

Recovering, Jessie greeted him cordially. "Hello, Errol!"

" 'Lo, Jessie. You've certainly grown up since I last saw you."

"I can say the same about you. But how . . . ?"

"I didn't escape, if that's what you're wondering." Only a couple of years older than Jessie, Errol had light yellow hair and dark blue eyes and a drawn and tight-lipped face. There was nothing bright about him at the moment except those eyes. Even in the dimness of the hospital room, Jessie could fancy that his eyes gleamed, like the eyes of a mountain cougar. "But never mind me. How're things goin' aboard the *Snohomish*?"

Jessie hesitated, glancing back at Errol's bedridden father, noting, as she had ever since her first visit here, the deep lines time had chiseled in his face. The doctors had told Moses Laird he might not survive the previous operation, that the chances were all against a man who had abused his stomach almost a lifetime. After the operation they had prophesied that Laird had one chance in a hundred of pulling through, but somehow he'd managed to hang on. Still, she feared the Ol' Boss would fret away what chance he did have if he learned of Captain Belluche's injuries and

20

the predicament Oceana was in as a result. So she decided against telling, at least for the present, and recounted the rest of the news as optimistically as possible, concluding, "And Ki managed to dump Fantan Monger overboard and to knock out Jack Wing and another man who was backing them."

"Monger and Wing, eh?" The significance wasn't lost on Moses Laird. "Boone Vermillion won't be far off." He dozed off a moment.

"We better leave," Errol urged. "Dad's very tired."

"Stick around," Moses Laird whispered. "There's things to be said." Another period of silence; then: "Good man, Ki. I won't worry so much knowin' Ki's goin' north with you. A-And Jessie, don't f'get the Laird code, takin' care of the loyal boys, and helpin' the deservin'—as long as they're deservin'. Don't go. Wait!"

Again Moses Laird appeared to be sleeping, but Jessie knew he was trying to organize his poor, bewildered brain.

"Seems like I had a bad dream," the Ol' Boss said at last. "Boone Vermillion was standin' by the bed. He was as near to laughin' as I ever saw him. 'So you thought you'd keep us from knowin' you had a stomach opperation, Laird?' he says. 'Why, we've been watchin' you all winter. Knew it was comin'. We never beat you Lairds, but with your son rottin' in jail, we'll beat anyone who tries takin' your crew north this season. Includin' Starbuck. And that'll hurt you more!' Then an orderly chased him away. Funny, how real dreams are. But he was right, blast him; if them two-legged wolves pulled you down, Jessie, nothin' could hurt me worse."

"I won't let them," Jessie assured him.

"Fight 'em," Laird urged. "And if Oceana goes down, I won't mind, just as long as it goes down fightin'. Lordy!

21

Lordy, I'd like to see the fight. Come back this fall and tell me about it."

Now Errol, glancing worriedly at Jessie, grasped his father's hand. "Sure, sure, Dad. You take it easy now," he said gruffly to cover his emotion. "S'long."

"S'long, cub . . . Jessie," Laird answered. His eyes followed Errol and Jessie through the door, as if for once he was admitting this might be the last time he would see them.

Closing the door behind them, Jessie remarked, "Any other man would have been dead, Errol, but your father thinks only of living."

"Some of the grub he ate in the early days was pretty terrible," he replied. "Jessie, I caught your hesitation in there just now. What's wrong? Or should I ask, what *else* is wrong?"

Jessie gave him a brisk account of Belluche's misfortune, watching his face darken in stiff, clotted rage. "Easy now, Errol. It won't do anybody any good for you to fly off the handle," she cautioned. "What we need now is someone to pilot the *Snohomish*. Can you take over as captain?"

"You don't believe in preliminaries, do you?"

"There isn't time."

"Time enough to clear a few things up first."

"Of course, Errol."

"Your dad and mine fought big money, big politicians, and fish pirates for the Glacier Inlet cannery," he said. "No man in the North was a better salmon hunter than my dad, even if I do say it."

"No question there," Jessie agreed. "Father always told me that Ol' Boss Laird could locate a school quicker than any man he ever saw."

"He tried to pass his knowledge along to me," Errol continued. "While you were going to private academies

22

and travelin' Europe, I was growin' up and workin' about the cannery, learning the operation from the ground up, and out in every kind of sea, handling every type of salmon catching gear."

"Go on," Jessie said.

"Last year I piloted the *Hecate* north, like I'd done plenty of seasons afore. The night she sank, we were in a making sou'wester, but she'd been built to withstand anything the coast could offer. Instead, unexplainably, she fell apart like a house o' cards in a wind. We launched the lifeboat, naturally, but it was just a gesture in that storm. There was a rescue, too, at last—for a few of us. It'd been better if I'd taken the old way, the never-come-back way, and perished with the *Hecate*. The coast guard's court of inquiry was as puzzled as myself about the cause, but I was captain, and when it was all over I was made to look pretty bad. Gross dereliction counts as a felony, so I got sent to the pen. This year, when my dad was told he might not pull through his operation, I went before the parole board and pleaded for clemency. Well, for his sake, I was paroled."

"And you came here to find out how he was."

"That's right, Jessie. And I found him with his chin up as usual, and the doctors giving him one chance in a hundred."

"You'll have to leave him if you're going to captain the *Snohomish*."

"I know, but Dad would likely rise up and kill me if he learned I'd turned you down. No, I want you to think it through. I'd be starting with two strikes against me," Errol said bluntly. "I'm an ex-con. The dereliction charge is still a club over my head. My trials and payin' for damages cleaned out our savings. I don't mind admittin' I'm pretty desperate, Jessie, but I'll never let you down. If you trust

23

me, I'll go to hell for you. But if you can't feel the same about me because of what's happened, then there's no deal and I'll go back and finish my time."

Jessie realized Errol Laird must be desperate or he wouldn't have gone into detail over his troubles. As a kid, she recalled, Errol had been a good-natured, towheaded tyke, lively with humor. The man before her was nervous and suspicious of everyone and their motives, intent on surrounding himself with protection. He looked much older than his mid-twenties age. Less than a year in prison had changed him. She estimated that normally he'd be around one hundred and ninety, two hundred pounds; now, he couldn't have weighed more than a hundred and sixty, wringing wet.

"Errol," she said, "you've got the wrong slant on things. I haven't lost faith in you. But you've lost faith in people. Ki and I need a captain, and somebody to help keep the wolves off our backs when the fighting gets tough. You're elected. Have I made it clear?"

A heavy sigh came from Errol's very depths, and something of a grin appeared. "You Starbucks are regular."

"Then get your gear aboard," Jessie declared. "Move into the captain's quarters, then cast an eye over the men we've taken aboard. There's a number of new faces, and I want to toss troublemakers back onto the dock before we sail."

On their way out of the hospital they ran into the orderly again. Jessie stopped the orderly, asking, "Sorry to bother you, but by any chance do you know if a stranger visited Moses Laird last night or the night before?"

"Sort of," the orderly answered after a moment's thought. "I do remember such a gent late yesterday evening. Saw him first in the sunroom at the end of the hall. Several patients were very low and I thought he was a relative. He smoked

24

and read and seemed to be nervous. I crossed the hall to the kitchen. When I returned, he was standing near the bed, staring at Mist' Laird and talking in a low voice. He was very polite. He explained he had heard Mist' Laird cry out, like in his sleep, and had looked in to see how he was gettin' along. Of course I reported the matter to the doctor."

"Thanks," Jessie said, and when the orderly was out of earshot, she told Errol: "Your father thinks it was a dream. Let's let him think that."

Jessie wasn't surprised Vermillion had invaded the hospital to learn Moses Laird's condition. And having discovered just how poor a shape Laird was in, Vermillion had lost no time in attempting a takeover. His first move had been to plant Jack Wing and Fantan Monger aboard the steamer. When that hadn't worked, he'd arranged an "accident" to stop the steamer from sailing, even if it meant the lives of Jessie and Captain Belluche. It came within a hair of succeeding, and it certainly would not be his last attempt. What would his next move be? When would he strike?

Long years of experience had taught Moses Laird how to meet such attacks. He'd always been prepared and difficult to surprise, for he'd usually anticipated the form the attack would take. His son Errol had some experience in seafaring, but most of it still lay ahead of him, as the *Hecate* tragedy seemed to indicate. And though his father had taught him much in cannery management, there hadn't been time to train him against surprise attack. Capt'n Errol was an unknown quantity, perhaps a loose cannon on deck, Jessie realized, and unfortunately neither she nor Ki was knowledgeable enough in this business to take up the slack. The odds for defeat, for outright disaster, were high.

★

# Chapter 3

It was still raining, with a gusting wind now blowing in from the southeast, as Jessie and Errol Laird returned to the wharves. Jessie pointed out the warehouse where she and Captain Belluche were almost killed by the falling barrels, and she related how she had confronted Hank Pierce, the suspect manager of the warehouse.

Listening, Laird eyed the building and then cast his eyes farther along the dock, to where a steamer was berthed—the *Ikatan Queen*, according to her bow nameplate. The ship was a slightly larger version of the *Snohomish*, newer, fresh-painted in white with a navy blue trim, her pilothouse pointed in gilt, and a gold outline of a mermaid adorning her stack. Husky roustabouts were stumbling and toiling up the sloping gangplank with their heavy loads. Aboard, crewmen were laboring to prepare the steamer for departure, which by all appearances was only a matter of hours away.

Without warning, Laird abruptly headed for the steamer. Jessie hastened to follow the impulsive man, aware he was in a wicked humor. He brushed savagely against several stevedores when they didn't move fast enough to get out of his path. And his ill humor seemed to turn to hot rage when he stalked up the gangplank and nearly collided with the man who had been occupying his—and Jessie's—thoughts.

In almost a snarl Errol acknowledged the man: "Vermillion."

Boone Vermillion was a dark-faced, dark-eyed individual. In his early forties, perhaps, he was a match for Errol in height and weight, but he carried the weight in a deceptive fashion and seemed a good twenty pounds lighter. There was a smooth, refined look about him, and he was weather-protected in an expensive Laxette worsted gray coat, with just the legs of his striped trousers showing below, stuffed in the tops of waterproof boots.

Noted for his financial power and influence in Seattle, Vermillion had an easy, affable manner. But his smile came too readily, Jessie thought; there was something evil and false behind that broad-lipped smirk.

"That was a narrow escape you had, Miss Starbuck," Vermillion greeted, totally ignoring Errol Laird. "I wish Captain Belluche had been as fortunate as you." His eyes were an indeterminate shade of gray. But as often as he smiled—and he was smiling now—the smile never reached those gray, fathomless eyes. "I'm sorry—"

"Sorry they weren't killed?" Laird interrupted sharply. There was no compromise in his manner and none in his voice.

Vermillion remained unruffled, continuing to smile. Only his eyes showed a betraying change of temper. "So, the jailbird has returned to his roost, strutting as ever," he said smoothly, then returned to Jessie. "You're

28

upset and you've reason to be, Miss Starbuck, but it was an accident. It could've happened to—"

Again Errol Laird cut in. "You're not foolin' anyone, Vermillion. If Oceana fails this season, you can pick it up cheap, something you've wanted to do for a long time."

"I admit I want the company. I figure combined, I can run your salmon cannery and my Mermaid Brand cannery more economically, and I've got the capital to back me. I made your pa a fair offer more'n once, too."

"Fair offer be damned. Oceana is worth twice what you wanted to pay." Errol narrowed his eyes, his voice dropping a notch. "I'll tell you your trouble. You're greedy for power and money. You've dabbed your claws into everything that wasn't nailed down. You own the biggest fishin' operation along the Northwest coast mainly because you froze out your competitors."

Vermillion's heavy, muscular hand stroked his smoothly shaved jaw. The hair-covered fingers of that strong hand came up past his lips to shield a portion of his continuous bland smile. "I practice good business, Laird."

"When you stoop to attempted murder, that's business of another color."

"You mean—?"

"I mean that was no accident when the rope sling hauling up those barrels broke in front of your warehouse. Miss Starbuck was slated to be the victim. Only Captain Belluche's quick move saved her, and for that he may die or be crippled for life. I don't know. But I'm holding you fully responsible for his condition."

For the first time the smile left Vermillion's features. The deep cleft in his chin became more pronounced as the skin tightened and stretched over the wide bones. "If I were you," he warned softly, "I wouldn't repeat that kind of talk around. I'll break you in short order if you do."

29

"Like you've broken others? Like you've already tried to break me?" Laird demanded harshly. "It wasn't weather that broke apart the *Hecate*, and we both know it!"

Vermillion's next move was as swift as it was unexpected. It caught Laird totally unprepared. Vermillion took a long stride forward and his left arm was swinging around in a vicious hooking blow in the midst of that stride.

"Watch out!" Jessie cried.

Too late. The blow rammed into Laird's short ribs, bringing his arms down in an instinctive motion. He never had a chance to avoid the short, jolting right-hand punch that crashed against the side of his jaw. He took two staggering steps backward, his feet sliding out from under him on the slippery deck. He lost his balance and went skidding and rolling down the gangplank, the uneven puncheons jabbing painfully into his spine. He was toppling toward the edge with the Seattle harbor a blue-green, scummy expanse below him, when his fingers found a hold on a plank and halted his fall.

Somewhere along the wharf a man yelled. The call was taken up by others. Boots pounded along the planking as the ship's crew and those ashore began converging, Jessie at the fore. But those seemed to be indistinct sounds to Errol Laird; he rose to his feet groggily and stood wavering, shaking his head to clear his senses. Then hunching his shoulders, he started back up the gangplank. He took his time. Not once while talking had he matched Vermillion's smile. But now Jessie saw him grin. But the gesture did nothing to soften his features. They remained rock-hard and implacable.

Fists bunched, long arms swinging, Laird approached the smiling Vermillion. Neither man seemed aware that the roustabouts had stopped their work, that a crowd was gathering along the wharf.

"Y'know, jailbird," Vermillion said, "that felt good."

Laird reached the deck and charged. Vermillion shifted his weight to one side. Laird's left slid past Vermillion's neck, but the right cross that followed it hit him under the left ear and shook him up.

"So did that," Laird gritted.

Then they lit into each other, two giants slugging away with both hands. The only sound was the vicious thudding of their fists against flesh and bone.

A jolting left drew blood from Laird's nose. But Laird opened a cut under Vermillion's eye, then slammed in fast, his arms pumping blurs. He bulled right through a smother of blows, taking them with a savage and willful pleasure, Jessie thought, just to land punches of his own. He slid a left in under the heart, then drove Vermillion to the rail with two slashing rights. The second of these rights bent Vermillion half over the rail. Before he could recover, an uppercut that started from the region of Laird's knees lifted Vermillion clear over the rail.

The result, Jessie reckoned, was more spectacular and satisfying than Ki's dumping of Fantan Monger overboard. With a foghorn bellow of shock and rage, Vermillion hurtled down past the slanting gangplank and struck the murky water in a geysering belly flop.

Surfacing almost immediately, gasping and blowing, Vermillion awkwardly struck out for the wharf, hampered by his coat. Eager hands were ready to rescue him. Someone let down a length of rope. Vermillion grabbed it and was hauled out, while a knot of seven or eight men gathered around him protectively. Among them Jessie noted Hank Pierce and others of Vermillion's hardcase warehouse workers. They formed a tight wedge behind their dripping boss as he glared up at Laird and strode toward the gangplank.

Laird turned slightly and grinned at Jessie, then eyed

31

Vermillion again. Roustabouts hastened to get out of Vermillion's path. Mud and brackish water soaked his coat and striped pants and squished from the soles of his boots.

"You look purty," Laird told him.

Vermillion's face was pale.

Behind Vermillion, Hank Pierce was an ugly, preying force. "Just say the word, Chief, and we'll blow Laird wide open. All I ask is a chance at the gal."

"Shut up." Vermillion waved him back. "I'll handle this." He climbed the gangplank and stopped in front of Laird. Laird lifted his fists, ready to continue the fight. But Vermillion shook his head and smiled. This time Jessie noticed the smile came with distinct effort.

"Remember me this way, Laird," he said slowly. He spoke calmly, but the heat of a tremendous consuming passion throbbed in the words. Vermillion was not a man to take a beating easily, especially one in public. The curious eyes of the crowd rankled deeply within him, put steel in his glance. "You may never have another chance," he added. "I'd settle this right now by killing you if I wasn't so set on getting to my Mermaid cannery."

A sense of wariness came over Laird. "If you're plannin' any booger play whilst we're sailin' north—"

"Hell, you're worse than an old woman," Vermillion scoffed. "But once this season is over and we're back here, I'll come looking for you with a gun. You savvy?"

"I savvy," Errol Laird said eagerly, the violence within him clearly straining to be unleashed. "Just you say the word.

Leaving the *Ikatan Queen*, Errol Laird had Jessie stop with him at a nearby dry-goods emporium, where he bought a duffel bag and supplies. Or rather, Jessie bought them for him; his probationary release from jail had come without money or personals. But he didn't seem to need much—

32

razor, knife, a couple of changes of clothes. Whatever else he needed, Laird assured Jessie, he carried in his head and in his two fists.

When they arrived at the *Snohomish*, the last of the cargo was going into the holds and the steamer was riding low in the water. Laird dumped his duffel in what had been Captain Belluche's cabin—paint-sick, musty, and shabby as the rest of the ship—and went out to meet with the old hands. Prominent among them were First Mate Hawser Yokum and Chief Engineer Chinook Norris, loyal crewmen who had been with Ol' Boss Laird since the founding of Oceana. Yokum was a chunky man, partly bald, wizened from long years spent in the out-of-doors. Norris was barrel-chested, with wicked gorilla arms, a scraggly gray mustache, yellowing at its untidy edges, covering his long upper lip. Both men bore the scars of countless dock brawls and free-for-all gangplank battles.

Yokum lifted his brows in surprise as he noted Errol Laird's bruised face. Laird explained what had happened.

"Your pappa found guns, fists, and clubs convenient in his time, but I hoped that day was over," Yokum grumped. "Did you beat Vermillion or was it a draw?"

"I won," Laird admitted. "Does that help my credit?"

"It don't hurt none," Yokum replied and laughed.

The loading continued apace. Jessie stayed out of the way, and out of the rain, conferring with Ki. They watched the stevedores and roustabouts truck lift-boards stacked with freight to points within reach of the ship's tackle. There was a lot of freight. Glacier Bay was located far from an Alaskan town, requiring the Oceana cannery to be self-contained during the operating season. Food, clothing, first aid, kerosene, machinery replacements, as well as hundreds of thousands of knocked-down cans had to be carried north.

In the rainy-gray, premature dimness at sunset, Jessie noticed the *Ikatan Queen* steaming out of the harbor. Vermillion's line flag streamed straight aft from the bow staff and the golden mermaid on her stack sent the waning rays of sun stabbing back at her. Somehow it made the *Snohomish* seem even more shabby. But the sight spurred the hands to greater effort, the gap in time closing between the two ships to a matter of a few hours, Errol Laird estimating their sailing time to be around midnight.

Shortly before midnight Jessie, Ki, and Capt'n Errol were making plans for their departure when Hawser Yokum approached with a grim expression. "Heard somethin'," he told Laird, gesturing dockside. "Sounded like trouble, if'n you ask—Damn! There it is again!"

They listened intently . . . and heard it. The sullen beat of heavy boots.

"Hell! We got ourselves a boardin' party coming!" Laird snapped. "Hawser—"

But Hawser Yokum was already darting off to rally the old hands, the ones he knew he could count on. Chinook Norris strode to the door of the engine room, spoke gruffly, and led four bent stokers to the deck, each armed with a club. They ranged along the rail, waiting with grim impatience while deckhands obeyed Laird's crisp injunction to draw in the plank.

The gangplank slid in and the pound of boots grew louder. A blot of men, dark against the wet, black curtain of night, took shape along the dock.

"Remember the chief's orders, boys," a harsh voice called. "Clean them snakes off'n the *Snohomish*, an' if they show fight, get down an' wreck the engines. Aw' ri', fly at 'em!"

The blot seemed to dissolve, spread out. There was a rush of attackers, the rasp of expelled breath, and they hurled themselves into the water on either side of the prow. Gimper Tynes unstrapped his wooden leg, swung it savagely against a head rearing over the deck line. The head vanished. With a surge the attackers swarmed over the fender wale. And every one of the old hands was battling—as well as Ki, who drove a foot into a contorted face, smashing back into the water. Chinook Harris swung a huge wrench, almost decapitating one of the boarders. But the attackers, outnumbering the defenders two to one, put a dozen men on the steamer despite the sturdy efforts of the club-swinging hands.

A man hurled himself at Capt'n Errol, and the younger Laird's yell was wild and joyous as he met the charge head-on with swinging fists. Flesh crashing against flesh, both men went down, rolling along the deck, pummeling each other savagely. Ki lifted an assailant bodily, juggled him in his arms, and hurled him far out into the harbor, where he hit with a splash. Jessie effectively laid waste with a hardwood rope pin. Curses, howls, and the wicked impact of clubs crashing against flesh-and-bone targets.

In a solid fighting line the old hands stood shoulder to shoulder against the Vermillion hirelings, driving them back, inch by inch, until only the rail and the water lay between them. Laird, wearied and spent from his efforts to prevent the takeover of the *Snohomish*, clung to the rail, catching his breath as he urged his crew on with encouraging words.

One of the hard-pressed Vermillion men flashed a gun, the muzzle flame dancing in the rainy gloom. Ki swore savagely, chopped the man with a calloused edge of his hand. And then, with Capt'n Errol leading, the crew swept the surviving invaders off the steamer.

Not until then was there a break in the ranks of the old hands. Errol Laird whirled from the bow, scurrying up the

35

ladder, yelling back, "Chinook, you warthog, leave the fightin' to them as can fight and look to your engines. Best way to finish this argument is to start steamin'!"

Chinook Norris didn't answer or delay. Breathing hard, he vanished in the dull glare of the boiler fires. There was a hiss of steam. Laird shouted the order to cast off the mooring lines. Deep within her the *Snohomish* throbbed to life. Slowly she backed from the slip, swinging her nose out into the harbor toward Puget Sound.

Shouts ran along the deck. Answering curses came from dripping attackers and their reinforcements on the dock. Gunfire slashed the night, the bullets thudding ominously into the superstructure. Pistols blazed a wicked reply from the decks, then there was nothing except the *humpa-thumpa, humpa-thumpa* of the engines, the song of escaping steam, and the increasing hiss of the bow wave.

Quivering with the reaction of it, Capt'n Errol braced himself against the rail, watching with Jessie and Ki the lights of Seattle fall behind. The virus of excitement, pride, and satisfaction helped to sustain him in this moment of physical letdown. They were northbound. Hawser Yokum was piloting up yonder at the wheel. Chinook Norris, as good an engineer as could be found, was at the throttle. A grizzled crew, reveling in the taste of victory, sniffed hungrily as the ship gathered way.

Ahead lay trouble, almost certainly, yet here was a good ship and yonder was the start of a fine salmon season. Laird grinned optimistically at Jessie and Ki; he was captain again, with a crew that had proved their loyalty and worth.

"God helping me," he commented to Jessie, "I won't let Dad or them down."

★
# Chapter 4

Clearing Puget Sound, the *Snohomish* dipped to a slow swell in the Strait of Juan de Fuca, cleaving it at eight knots, a white bone in her teeth. The glow of small port towns made lucent arcs across the sky far astern. The strait spread dark and silent, boundaried by mountains with their wooded feet laved by the ocean and bare granite heads among the cloud-hidden stars.

Enchanting waters lay ahead. From Olympia, Washington, to Skagway, Alaska, there were a thousand miles of water protected from storms by a mountain range on the easterly side and mountainous islands on the westerly. Twice the sea broke through to remind the traveler that the Pacific was turbulent. The route was known as the Inland Passage, and there were spots where a man could stand on deck and throw a stone to the shore.

Errol Laird, Jessie knew, had traversed the Inland Passage as long as he could remember. Yet, as he remarked to her, he'd never tired of the sight of the mighty cedars and firs of Washington and British Columbia stretching from water's edge far up the slopes of the brooding mountains. And intent on making fast time to the cannery, Laird took to sailing all night that first night, and on subsequent nights whenever weather and moonlight permitted. Being well acquainted with all the vagaries of the changing sea channel, he pushed on relentlessly, driven by a nameless feeling of uneasiness that grew with each passing day.

And driven as well by infrequent glimpses of a ship far ahead. The mermaid-gilded funnel of the *Ikatan Queen* would loom tauntingly in the distance, gliding swiftly northward, egging Laird to try and catch her if he could.

Then, for a stretch, heavy rains set in, sodden downpours bringing gloomy days, black nights and a choppy sea, its swollen breast gorged with dirt. Before the rains had passed, the rudder jammed. The steamer slewed in mid-channel and drove prow-deep into the muddy shoreline. No real harm was done except to slow an already slow upstream passage. After that the engines failed twice, seemingly without cause. Hawser Yokum muttered about "ol' devil trouble, he sure ride the Laird boats." But Capt'n Errol made no bones about suspecting some of the new hands of what he called "malicious scamping."

Busy as he was between bunk and the pilothouse, Laird found time for conversing with Jessie. It seemed to warm his blood, the vision of her golden-green mysterious eyes, the gentle curve of her fair-skinned cheek, her red lips, mobile and lovely, her softly modulated voice and the graceful movements of her body. And he had no way of knowing how his own presence—his strong, rugged face, his powerful, well-proportioned body, the turbulent spirit so evident in everything he said and did—affected Jessie Starbuck.

When she was with Laird, she was filled with a wildness, an abandon, as though some headlong and kindred spirit linked them together. In a sense, perhaps, one did, considering they'd known each other as young children. Yet because she was a strong and willful woman, and had a sharp sense of pride, as well as of business etiquette, Jessie insisted upon freezing out all the disturbing sensations that sought to sway her emotions.

There was no amusement in her eyes, only a strange brilliance that might have been warmth and tenderness, the night when Jessie joined Laird on the bridge. After acknowledging her with a smile, he turned his slicker up about his ears and stared intently ahead. The rain had tapered off, at least temporarily, and the stars were out and it was growing colder. Lights of small settlements and lone cabins shone vaguely on either shore. Here people wrested a living from the timber or the sea. It was a land of few roads and vast areas of unexplored territory—the last frontier.

"What's the weather ahead?" Jessie asked. She was afraid of fogs and delay, knowing that when fog grew too thick, Capt'n Laird had to drop hook and wait. They might ride at anchor for several days, and time was important.

"Weather's cold and clear," Laird answered. "I'm driving her hard now, to make slack water in Seymour Narrows."

Dour Duncan McArdle happened to come by just then, accompanied by Ki. Stopping, they discussed conditions aboard ship for a moment, then McArdle asked: "Capt'n, what kind of cannery job have you in mind for me this year?"

"I was going to use you as a pinch hitter. Why?"

"I was thinking," McArdle said slowly, "if Boone Vermillion is out to get you, he'll strike at the fish trap. I'd like to take a whirl at a trap guard's job."

"You're asking for a lot of trouble, Duncan."

"Aye, Capt'n. Do I get the job?"

"You can have just about anything you want," Laird replied.

Pleased, Duncan McArdle left, going below. Ki stayed and asked what a trap guard was.

"We have fish traps," Laird explained. "Every so often the traps are lifted and the salmon dumped into scows and brought to the cannery. The traps don't supply enough fish, of course, so we buy some salmon from the trollers. Unless the traps are guarded, fish pirates, operating as trollers, raid the traps and sell us our own fish. Guards," he added significantly, "don't last long."

"Why?"

"Either they sell out to the pirates and I find out about it, or the pirates run them off the trap. Whichever—" Laird suddenly paused, interrupted by the telegraph jangling at his side; then the port engine stopped. Laird swore softly and, with a concerned glance at Jessie and Ki, waited for an explanation to come up the speaking tube.

Instead, a few minutes later Chinook Norris himself clattered up the stairs. The engineer's hands were kneading a ball of cotton waste aimlessly and his face was lined with exasperation. "Lube oil line let go," he said. "We'll be shut down for a while on the one engine."

Laird frowned. "Serious?"

"I don't know yet," Norris answered. "I think I caught it in time. But it isn't that. I was in the messroom when I heard 'er pounding, and I sensed she was running hot. Petrovsk, the first assistant, was on watch. I got below quick. Another few seconds and she'd be burned out for certain. A shipyard job."

"I thought there was a warning whistle on the lubricating system," Laird said.

Norris wiped one hand, then the other on his soiled boiler suit. "That's just it, Cap. The pressure valve operatin' the whistle was plugged closed. So was the lube oil line. Nasty business." He glanced toward Jessie and Ki, unsure whether he should voice or not.

"Go ahead," Jessie said tersely. "Nothing you can add would be shocking after what we've run into so far."

"Yes'm. Capt'n, there's somebody on this steamer who doesn't want to see Glacier Bay in a hurry—if at all. I know who it is, but I don't know why, or how or who's working with him, I—"

He stopped as Frenchie Tabac came up the stairs. The second mate was brushing crumbs from his sweater. The skin on both hands, between thumb and forefinger, was stained with lube oil and kerosene.

Laird's voice was tight. "You helping out the black gang these days?"

Tabac grinned weakly. "I'm something of a basement mechanic, y'know," he replied. "I was tuning the galley range."

Laird said, "I think it's time that the crew of this kettle start keeping their noses out of other folks' departments and pay more attention to their own. And that goes for me." He faced Norris. "Okay, Chinook, see what you can do with the port engine. Meanwhile, drop the starboard one down to slow. Just enough to keep us steady on course."

Tabac departed. Norris paused before leaving, remarking after Tabac was out of earshot: "He's French-Canadian. I got nothin' against Canucks, but that guy I don't care for. He don't look like no deep-water mate; he looks like a shoe clerk. Not a very good shoe clerk at that."

"The *Snohomish* needed a second mate," Laird replied with a shrug. "The hiring hall must've checked Tabac out as a second mate when they sent him over, and Captain Belluche must've been satisfied when he hired him on. You'll have to learn to like him."

"No," Norris said, "you're wrong. I don't gotta like him. Maybe I can't fire him, but I can watch him." He jerked his quilted cap down over his eyes and headed back to the engine room.

Sighing, Laird called over to the helmsman, "She's all yours," and then turned and smiled wearily at Jessie and Ki. "Well, who's for a brandy nightcap?"

Ki looked at Jessie, his eyes questioning, then responded, "Best I turn in. Good night, all."

After Ki had left, Laird canted his head and regarded Jessie. "And as for you, Miss Starbuck?"

"As for me, Captain Laird, you may see me to my room."

"It's the least I can do." Taking her arm, he guided her the few steps to her door. But instead of stopping, he continued along with her in tow, her arm still engaged.

"What—?"

"I told you it was the least I could do," Laird said. "It's certainly not as much as I *can* do." He steered her for another twenty feet, and through the door of his captain's quarters. After releasing her, he slid the bolt on the door, set up glasses, filled them from a cut-glass decanter, removed his coat, handed his apprehensive guest a glass, and said, "Sit!"

Jessie glanced around. "Where?"

"Take your choice. There're two chairs and a bed."

That was true—as far as it went. The bed was bunk-size, a tight fit for a man of Laird's proportions. The chairs were hardback, small, and skinny like the bed. They fit the cramped confines of the cabin, however, which contained only a few other furnishings—a fold-down chart table, a wardrobe, and chest of drawers, a brass-cased chronograph, a liquor cabinet, and a mirrored washstand.

Jessie opted for the bed. Not because it was suggestive of any budding desires—which there were, she had to admit. For all of her sense of propriety between Captain Laird and herself, she could also sense a perverse little tingling beginning between her thighs, as though her sensuality was responding to his masculine challenge. No, she picked the bed because whatever was going to happen between them would no doubt be preceded by some relentless moving about, and she wanted maneuvering room not provided by the seat of a chair.

Laird sipped from his glass and stared down at her, a hotness to his gaze. "This smacks of the *Hecate* sinking."

"Perils of the sea," Jessie murmured noncommittally.

"Forget that perils of the sea stuff. I've been over that before—with the coast guard. It wasn't weather broke the *Hecate* apart. I like at least an even break when I go to sea, not loaded dice."

"So you're convinced your ship was rigged to sink?"

"Yeah, but I can't prove it." He sat down gingerly on the bed, cleared his throat. "If I could, I'd sleep better nights."

Jessie stared at him, feeling his warm presence—stared at the broad outline of his shoulders and chest through his shirt, his long muscular arms, the flat hardness of his belly. She felt a rising tendril of passion coiling up from her loins, hardening her nipples . . . and then, with a sultry glance lower, she grew achingly aware of the thickening bulge straining against his trousers. Her mouth, her lips swelling in anticipation, formed his name.

43

"Errol . . ."

Their gazes met, locked. A pause lengthened.

"E-Errol," she finally stammered, trying to regain her composure. "Why didn't you speak up at the investigation?"

Laird smiled bitterly. "I had other things on my mind along about that time. Like how a man looks when he's washed up on a beach after a week or so in the water. There were five of them, Jessie. Five." He placed a hand on her knee and went on: "Since then I've had time to wonder about it. A lot of time. Like when I'm lying awake nights waiting for sleep to come."

He lapsed into lame silence, and another paused developed, each aware of the other and enormously stirred by nearness and feeling. And in that electric moment, Jessie knew she was no longer reluctant, that her blood was filled with a fire that flamed through her flesh and goaded her to reckless abandon.

"Errol," she purred, "if you dare try to kiss me . . ."

He stiffened as if she'd read his mind. "Y-yes?"

"If you do, then I won't dare to try kissing you first."

There was an impact as their bodies crushed in an embrace, her arms curling around his neck, her tingling breasts pressing against his chest, her mouth insistent and bruising against his. He moaned slightly, deep in his throat, his hands gliding down her back to stroke her tensing buttocks through her pants. Jessie found that she was moaning a little, too.

His hands then gently and firmly began to undo her blouse. "You have too many clothes on," he murmured, bunching the blouse higher, then slipping it over her head and off her upraised arms. He stared at her breasts, exclaiming, "B'gawd, have you growed up, Jessie." He cupped them, his fingers kneading gently. His head bent,

44

his lips kissing and then suckling each distended nipple thirstily.

Jessie sighed, her head swaying back and forth. "You have too many clothes on, too," she gasped, her hands reaching for his trousers, fumbling to undo the buttons of his fly. Tender and gentle, her fingers drew out his erection and began to stroke its fleshy shaft. Still rubbing him with one hand, she used her other to push his pants down, until reluctantly, he had to stop nursing on her breasts and finish taking his trousers down. Furiously he stripped them off, along with his boots and shirt, then crawled onto his bed, one wildly aroused male.

Again his mouth engulfed each breast in turn, his tongue licking her nipples. Then he wandered lower, kissing her navel as, with her help, he unbuckled her pants and stripped her bare. His lips trailed lower until they were browsing on her naked loins, sliding back and forth, deeper, his tongue plunging into her.

Jessie shuddered, her breathing erratic, ragged. Her legs splayed wider, bending at the knees to give him fuller access. Her sensitive flesh felt Errol press his mouth closer. He was greedy and nibbling. His tongue was everywhere. Jessie swooned. A minute . . . two minutes . . . her belly rippled. She began to pant explosively. Her loins curved up, pressed with trembling tension to force that stroking tongue tighter to the vibrant center of her body.

And Jessie climaxed. She wailed and twisted in the grip of her sweet agony, her writhings never breaking with the tongue and lips that were consuming her in ecstasy. Then with a final stroke from bottom to top, Errol lunged up over her, and her hands clutched at his hardness, guiding it eagerly to the entrance of her empassioned hollow.

45

His thick goad stabbed into her. Jessie twitched, feeling impaled, an agony of pleasure that grew sharper and tighter the deeper he skewered into her. She could feel his pulse from it. Errol breathed through his mouth, hugging her, forcing his girth into her hot depths, her insides igniting as he buried all of his huge invader.

His strong movements began at once. Straining and pistoning, his buttocks flexing, he hammered into her in a savage lust that rocked them both with squirming convulsions. Jessie spread her thighs and clamped her legs around his heaving body, helping him sink fully to the hilt.

Their bodies gleaming with sweat, they began a slow, steady stroking. They heard the jingle of the telegraphs and the increasing vibration of the one steam engine picking up revolutions below, resonating through the bed. Matching tempo, Jessie rotated her hips, feeling her muscles clenching, milking him as he started to piston faster and faster within her. She climaxed again, humping hard against his groin, raking his bucking back with her nails, biting his chest, panting uncontrollably . . . and somewhere about that time, she sensed his own completion fast approaching. "Now, Errol, now . . ."

He slammed in and out of her violently, his mouth gasping out crazed entreaties. And then it was upon him, the explosion, his hot liquid fire rushing to jet far up inside her hungry belly. . . .

Drained of energy yet sensually alive, Jessie let her bent legs slide down limply on either side of Errol. He dropped forward, remaining locked between her pulsating thighs. Satiated, contentedly entwined, they dozed off . . .

Until suddenly, without warning, there erupted a muffled explosion from belowdecks, and the *Snohomish* shuddered violently, slewing about, once again dead in the water. . . .

46

Ki had not gone to bed.

What he'd told Jessie and Captain Laird had been an excuse, pure and simple, in order to politely exit. And it hadn't been solely for their sakes, either, though he had sensed their underlying desire to be alone. It had been for his own sake as well, to avoid that brandy nightcap. He didn't often drink liquor, hard or soft, and tonight he found himself in the mood for a large mug of seaman-style coffee—mud, boiled with eggshells and salt.

So Ki drifted down toward the galley. Crossing the main deck, bracing himself as the steamer lifted and rolled to the rising sea, he could hear the muted whisper of the wind sounding over and above the slow chuffing of the starboard engine, and could see foamy green water surging through the bow chocks and flooding aft along the deck. Descending belowdecks, he entered the messroom and enjoyed not one but two steaming mugs of "mud," passing the time jawboning with a few of the crew.

Leaving the messroom, heading along the companionway, Ki passed the midships hatchway that led down to the engine room. The hatch was ajar, and he chanced to glance through, down a short ladder to a steel-grated landing and catwalk. He could barely see a thing, for the landing was feebly illuminated by only one dim lantern, and it was enveloped in steam and smoke escaping from the boilers, pipes, and the hammering starboard engine deeper below. Yet he thought he glimpsed through the swirling murk the figure of a man—a man on his hands and knees, crawling, groping.

Startled, Ki was taking a fast second look—when suddenly from the depths of the engine room came a jarring detonation, wrenching the ship about, slamming Ki against the hatchway door. Recovering, yet still half-stunned, he leapt down the ladder, hearing cries of alarmed crewmen echoing along the companionway.

"Norris!"

The ship's engineer was almost unconscious. Blood trickled from both nostrils, seeping out of his mouth in a crimson froth.

Ki bent to help Norris, and the move quite likely saved his life. From out of the catwalk's thick gloom lanced gunflame; a bullet seared a furrow across the nape of his neck. Momentarily stunned, he sprang back against the bulkhead and went down. Faint light funneling along the catwalk glinted on the barrel of a .44 Smith & Wesson revolver. Rolling as the pistol targeted him for a point-blank shot, he launched himself at the shifting gunarm and his fingers closed on tensed tendons. The gunman kicked viciously at his ribs. Ki grunted but hung on and sunk his fingers into the wrist. He heard the revolver clatter to the catwalk.

He was up on his knees then and lashing out with stiffened fingers at the man's belly. His blow sunk deep and the man sagged spitting curses, backpedaling along the catwalk, his figure a black haze in the weak, smoky light. After kicking the fallen revolver off the edge of the catwalk, Ki pursued the man, leaping into the air after two springing strides, aiming with both heels for the man's gut again. He nearly missed, for his opponent spun smoothly to one side so Ki's right heel barely grazed a hip before he crashed into the guardrail and hit the catwalk hard but rolling.

In that instant Ki realized two things: One was that the man was the second mate, Frenchie Tabac—but that was less of a surprise than the other fact. The Canuck was a *savate* fighter, a damned leaper, possibly as fast and deadly with his feet as Ki himself. And even as Ki came

48

out of the roll into a crouch, his foe was on the attack, and not merely with his feet.

Lamplight glinted on a long, narrow blade that ended in a needle-thin point, the sort of knife known as an "Arkansas toothpick" in the American West. What it was called up in Canuck country, Ki neither knew nor cared. His sole interest in the weapon was keeping it from his flesh.

Ki, too, carried a blade—a *tanto*, a very short, delicately curved sword no bigger than a knife, really, and much shorter than his opponent's weapon—but he had no chance to draw it. Frenchie Tabac was instantly leaping at him, a booted foot slamming into the ridged, iron-hard muscles of his abdomen, bringing a grunt from him and slamming him backward against one of the support posts. Ki straightened to counterattack, feeling the post jab against his back through his shirt and leather vest, his fingers seeking the handle of the knife in his belt. But he barely had time to bob down and to the left as the long-bladed "toothpick" slashed upward, passing a fraction of an inch from his bicep.

As his foe spat out a curse, Ki made a blade-edge of his calloused left hand and slammed it down hard on the other's knife arm, bringing a howl of pain—but not before that slender knife was again flashing toward his throat. Ki sprang back and sent a savage kick to his attacker's midsection, and as Tabac was bent over by its impact, Ki tried for a killing blow to the base of the skull.

Tabac escaped death with a movement of no more than a fraction of an inch, and Ki's stiffened fingers buried themselves in muscle rather than bone. It still had effect. Tabac went sprawling, giving Ki a vital instant, which he used to draw his *tanto*. In a single fluid motion he whipped out the small sword and brought its edge across Tabac's exposed neck, severing his windpipe and jugular veins, which fountained blood as the Canuck toppled over.

Swiftly resheathing his *tanto*, Ki hurried back to Chinook Norris on the landing. Already footsteps were clanging hollowly down the steel ladder leading from the companionway hatch above, and glancing up, Ki saw Jessie and Capt'n Laird descending, with a pack of crewmen right behind. Momentarily ignoring them, he put hands under Norris's armpits, and the chief engineer got unsteadily to his feet.

"Tabac," Norris said thickly. Other hands reached to help, but he waved them away. "Got t'stop Tabac."

"He's stopped. He's dead," Ki assured him.

Norris picked up his cap, wincing as he tried to pull it onto his head. "I was just finishin' repairs on the port engine when I caught Tabac tamperin' with the starb'd engine. He came after me with a pistol, cracked me a good'n afore I could get away." Rubbing at the rising lump above his ear, he eyed Laird. "We got troubles, Capt'n. Number three and four bearings'll need shimming up. The Canuck did it up right proper."

"He did worse'n that," Laird said grimly. "All hell bust loose a few minutes ago, when you must've been knocked out colder'n a flounder. Skewed the ship around, and flung us clean out of be—er, our chairs. The starboard engine must've seized up, is my guess."

"The lousy, ship-scampin' son!" Norris raged. "It'll take a week to overhaul that engine!"

"And we don't have the time to spare," Jessie pointed out, feeling the cold retching of despair in her gut.

"We have no choice," Laird reminded her. "We're fairly close to Port Tenino, and assumin' the port engine and the weather holds steady, we'll be able to limp in on one lung. Let's just hope we can make up for the lost time when we reach the cannery at Glacier Bay." He glanced over at the dead body of Frenchie Tabac, then slammed his fist into his palm. "We may be down, but we ain't derelict yet! We may be a Company of the Damned, but dammit, we ain't licked yet!"

The hands packing the ladder and landing had never seen Capt'n Laird so gripped by emotion, and they caught up his spirit. For a moment they stared at him, then they jumped to work, as if stung by a lash. B'gawd, if the *Snohomish* was crewed by a Company of the Damned, they were going to hell fighting back!

★

# Chapter 5

Port Tenino was typical of the fishing and logging settlements that were scattered along the Inland Passage—at least, from a distance. As the crippled *Snohomish* approached the town, Jessie and Ki could make out a broad, crescent-shaped bay formed by the mouth of a fast-flowing river, which later they learned was called the Rogue. On the lee side of the Rogue was a harbor with a steamer landing and an anchorage for trollers; and strewn across the bank above appeared to be a motley hodgepodge of buildings, shacks, and tents, many of them clustered near a ramshackle lumber mill that fronted the river.

The *Snohomish* tied up alongside a float from which a gangway ran ashore. Immediately Capt'n Errol and all hands set to working like madmen, tearing down the starboard engine and replacing and repairing—with the aid of the crude machine shop run by the local blacksmith—the parts sabotaged by Frenchie Tabac. Jessie and Ki pitched in whenever and however they could, but on the morning of the second day they found enough time on their hands to go ashore on their own.

By now they had made enough trips from the steamer to town and back to conclude that Port Tenino was an isolated dump of a place—and worse. Somehow it exuded something else, a sense of menace that belied the honest activities of the fishermen, timberjacks, and their families who crowded the single main street. That feeling came from hombres with cold eyes and holsters, men who lounged with studied insolence against the saloon fronts. Gunhands. Jessie noted them as she had on previous visits, wondering what the attraction was about remote Port Tenino to turn it into a hardcase hangout.

Midway along the main street—and serving, in a sense, as the dividing point between the rough half and respectable half of town—was the one restaurant that wasn't inside a saloon. And saloons were male-only domains. Even so, the Victoria Café was scarcely more than a large, square room seemingly tacked on as an afterthought to the side of the Victoria Gentlemen's Club, with the hubbub from the bar echoing through their common wall and connecting doorway, adding to the loud talk of patrons at its stubby tables. It was not very crowded when Jessie and Ki entered, and they had no trouble finding an empty table. A paunchy man in a bib apron and dungarees came out from the back, scratching his hairy chest through the sides of his apron. Jessie ordered two roast beef sandwiches and coffee, the sandwiches and brew being standbys that most cafés would have fresh on hand. Shortly the man returned with their food, and Jessie paid him.

Eating, Ki idly scanned the room. Under a vapor of steam and smoke, a scattering of fishermen were wolfing down meals, having remained ashore for one reason or another after most of their mates had left aboard troll-ers before dawn. And there were a dozen or so lumber-jacks, readily identifiable in their flannel shirts, cord pants, and laced hobnail boots. There were also quite a few gentlemen wearing similar garb of the timberland, yet their hands, Ki felt sure, were not calloused by saws or axes.

"I've seen meaner ports," he remarked, "but barely."

"I could do with never seeing it again," Jessie added, then abruptly stiffened, eyeing a man who was coming through the connecting door from the saloon. "Speaking of seeing, Ki, maybe I'm seeing things. But isn't that the man who was with Jack Wing and Fantan Monger back in Seattle, the one who sided them when they tried boarding the *Snohomish*?"

Casting a glance at the man, Ki nodded. There was no mistaking the bewhiskered bruiser, particularly with his bulbous nose crisscrossed by a couple of dirty sticking plasters—the result, no doubt, of his nose-bashing fight with Ki. He, too, was dressed in logger's garb but wore high-heeled riding boots and an old Remington .44 sag-ging in a holster.

If the man happened to recognize Jessie or Ki, he gave no indication but continued threading between the tables to the front door and on outside. Silently they kept a sur-reptitious eye on him, watching through the grimy front window as he mounted a wiry grulla and headed slowly up the street. When he had passed from view, Jessie turned back to Ki, shaking her head.

"Seeing him here sure poses a bunch of questions."

"Well, it answers one," Ki said. "Soon as we docked, remember, we heard that Vermillion's *Ikatan Queen* had already come and gone a good day or more ahead of us."

Jessie nodded. "That's right. And Vermillion will gain at least a week's jump on us by the time we're ready to leave, if Chinook Norris's estimation is correct—a week in which Vermillion can set up that much more trouble for us."

"Point is, Jessie, we've been wondering whether Vermillion stopping here was just coincidence, or was he up to something we oughta worry about. Now, the only logical way that man could've gotten here was on the *Queen*, and seein' that he was left here makes me think Vermillion isn't waiting a week."

"And who else he's left behind," Jessie reflected, thinking of Wing and Monger. After finishing her sandwich, she gave a dainty little hiccup and said, "I feel like a new lady, Ki. What say we follow up on the man, see who and what else we can see. In the situation Laird is in, we can't afford to overlook any dangers, no matter how slim or against the odds."

Exiting the Victoria Café, they stared in the direction the man had ridden. There was no sign of him. Up thataway the street was lined with saloons, cribs, pawnshops, and other questionable establishments; down the street were tradesmen and stores, a post office, a fish-buyer's station, the blacksmithy, and a small livery stable. The man was no place to be seen along there, either, or just beyond where the street ended at the lumber mill.

Ki hunkered by the hitchrail where the man's grulla had stood. That particular spot seemed especially popular, all churned up with horse tracks, boot tracks, even dog tracks. Ki took his time studying the morass.

Watching him, Jessie commented, "Ki, I doubt anybody of the sort who'd know that man is going to tell us where he went."

56

"Likely not. Nobody may know, either, but it's worth a try." His patience paid off; he untangled a pattern that seemed to fit the size, weight, and general manner of the grulla. These prints he scrutinized minutely, then straightened. "The left foreshoe had a distinctive notch near its toe. If worse comes to worse, and we have to track the man out of town, I reckon I'll be able to recognize his horse's tracks anywhere now."

"Well, if we're going to go anywhere, then maybe I should arrange for a couple of horses for ourselves," Jessie said, gesturing toward the livery stable. "For that matter, while I'm at it, I'll see if he stabled his horse. If he hasn't, I can check the shops."

"Whereas a lady can't rightly check the barrooms," Ki added, pointing uptown. "I'll meet you back here."

They parted then, Ki angling for the nearest saloon while Jessie walked down the row of cheap storefronts to the livery. The man's grulla was not there, and the gabby old hostler couldn't recollect having ever stabled such a critter. To judge by his red-veined, bleary-eyed face, however, Jessie had sincere doubts that the hostler could've remembered much of anything past last night's bottle of rotgut. Among the cavvy of rental nags she found a couple of capable and relatively young mounts—a hock-scarred moro gelding for Ki, and a shaggy yet solid sorrel mare for her—which she paid the hostler to saddle with rental gear and have standing ready just in case.

In case of what, Jessie wasn't sure. She had a strange hunch, though, that it might well be something hellacious, and even if she were wrong, she felt better spending the money to have the horses than risk being caught later in need of them. Still keeping her notion of being prepared in mind, she bought boxes of extra ammunition for her pistol when she stopped in the hardware store. By then she had asked about the man and his grulla in a number of other shops, but she had discovered nothing, absolutely nothing for her trouble.

Returning to the livery, she packed the boxed ammunition in the saddlebag of her rental mare. As the hostler had assured her, the mare and Ki's gelding were saddled loose-cinched but otherwise ready. The hostler was nowhere around—or so it appeared at first. But then, as somewhat annoyed she was starting to leave the stable again, the hostler came rushing bandy-legged in through the double-doored front entrance, wagging his finger at her.

"Her! It's her!" he squalled. "Here she is!"

He was yelling to the two men who loomed in the doorway a step behind him. They both had revolvers in hand as they pushed the hostler aside and lunged toward Jessie. One was balding, with a seamed ferret face, and wore a faded checked shirt and muddy duck pants tucked into the tops of stiff knee-high boots. Jessie had never seen him before, but she sure as hell had seen the other—the last time when he'd ridden off aboard a wiry grulla.

With a snarl the all-too-familiar bewhiskered brute grabbed Jessie by the arm as she was pivoting to flee.

"Let go of me!" Jessie snapped, struggling against his grip, only to have her other arm snagged by the ferret-faced man. Pinned between them, she ceased resisting, though she continued glaring with haughty defiance. "How dare you! I'll have you whipped for this!"

"Gawd, but I hate yammery females," the bearded man rasped loudly and ripped Jessie's pistol out of her holster. Thrusting it behind his belt, he told her: "If you don't dry up, sister, I'll throttle you with my bare hands."

"Don't kill her!" the hostler quavered. "Not in my place!"

"Stop sniveling," the bearded man growled at him. "I ain't gonna kill her, less'n she forces me to. Factually, I don't know *what* to do with her, 'cept let her go. It ain't by no coincidence that she and her Chink laundryman eyeballed me in the Victoria and now's been snooperin' around town."

"They's up to somethin' f'sure, Unruh," the ferret-faced man agreed. "No question we gotta keep her, at least till we go tell Madigan. He's the only who can figure what to do with a feisty bangtail like her."

"Not here!" the hostler squawked. "You can't keep her—"

Releasing Jessie, the bearded man called Unruh back-handed the hostler across the face, knocking him to the ground. Ignoring the hostler, who sagged, dazed but silent, Unruh addressed the other man: "To the mill, Fowles." He scratched his beard as though mulling over options, then eyed Jessie malevolently. "Now we're all gonna take a nice friendly walk, and you're gonna act like a lady. 'Cause if you don't, if you act up, Your Ladyship ain't gonna *die* like a lady."

Flanked closely by the two gunmen, Jessie was marched out through the front of the stable. The hostler remained trembling inside, wiping the blood from his bruised jaw, as they stepped to the street and started down to the nearby lumber mill. Jessie glanced swiftly about but failed to spot Ki. There were plenty of other folks around, though, and her first impulse was to wrench free, try for the derringer hidden behind her belt buckle, and scream bloody murder. Yet bloody murder was what could all too easily happen— if not to her, then to some innocent bystander coming to help. Unruh and Fowles were definitely on the prod and

59

almost as nervous as the hostler.

Unlike the main street the grounds around the mill and along the river appeared deserted. Approaching the mill, they passed a pond and a drying yard, then entered the main building through a side door. And now, hidden from view, whatever risky chance Jessie might have had was lost. Her only hope was that Ki had managed to glimpse her in the street, but even assuming he had, he still wouldn't know where she was being taken.

Fowles thrust Jessie ahead of him, while Unruh struck a match and lit the wick of a tubular Dietz lantern. Even with the lamp glowing, the interior was gloomy, the only windows small-paned and high along the wooden walls. It stank of dryrot and was festooned with cobwebs, sawdust, and rodent droppings. Evidently it was currently being used as a storage room, for it was loaded from floor to ceiling with boxes, barrels, hand tools, and machine parts, with narrow paths for passageways burrowing through the clutter.

"You was a good gal," Unruh told Jessie snidely as he reached for some lengths of thin leather stripping that were hanging on a nail. He selected a couple of strips, then gestured for her to stand by one of the upright posts. "I don't reckon you'll last that way on your own, so I'm just gonna have to make sure you behave."

Again Jessie felt the impulse to resist, but again she swallowed her urge. Fowles was blocking the door, his revolver dangling in his grip—but it wasn't dangling *that* loosely, and she knew she'd never be able to draw her derringer before he gunned her down. And if not him, Unruh would get her.

Stifling her angry frustration and resentment, Jessie did as ordered. With her arms behind her and around the post, Unruh wrapped her wrists and knotted the thongs tightly.

"She ain't going nowhere now," he said to Fowles. "Watch her anyhow, and if she sets a-squawkin', feed her your kerchief." Then, with a final malicious grin, he unlatched the door and strode outside, slamming the door behind him.

Watching him depart, Jessie realized that Unruh might be the servant of two masters—Boone Vermillion in Seattle and someone local named Madigan. Which meant that although he was definitely a piece in the puzzle, how and where the bearded man fit in was a puzzle in itself. Yet, other than wondering about it and what was to come, Jessie was helpless. Fowles was leaning against the doorjamb, and with her hands bound behind her, she could do nothing except slump against the post and endure his rudely ogling stare. . . .

Meanwhile, Ki, having left Jessie at the Victoria Café, worked his way up the boardwalk from saloon to saloon. It was a good time to ask around, he thought; it was the dull morning hour long before the customary flurry of evening trade, and the bartenders, bored and logy, might just say something they wouldn't normally. However, he had no luck in the first handful of establishments, their bartenders and patrons tight of mouth, making it clear to strangers that they preferred strangers out the door.

He hit paydirt, though, at the largest of Port Tenino's saloons—a two-storied false-front sticking up from a row of one-story hovels like a festering thumb, its patch-painted siding looking like scrap lumber from some old dance hall. An arch over the entrance read THE ANTLER INN * J. J. MADIGAN, PROP. Among the horses lining the saloon's hitchrails was that elusive wiry grulla.

Entering, Ki found the Antler Inn to be a scene of contrasts. The woodwork was raw and unpainted, the long bar of roughly planed planks, yet the tables and chairs were polished smooth with age and use, and the backbar mirror was genuine French plate. Bottles of every shape and color pyramided the backbar, and the lunch counter over to one side gleamed with copper and glass.

Ki walked through the saloon, seeking the grulla's owner. Again, no luck. Rankled, he rechecked the saloon on the off-chance he'd overlooked the bearded man in a bathroom or some shadowy nook or cranny. But no man. Now, there was no guarantee that just because the man's horse was tied outside the Antler Inn that the man was inside the Antler Inn. But the man had been wearing high-heeled boots, Ki recalled, indicating he was a rider, not a walker. And by nature a rider wouldn't walk anywhere if he had a horse handy.

So, Ki reckoned, the odds were that the man was still within the saloon's building. Perhaps upstairs, perhaps someplace in back. Anyway, it was worth a search.

The second floor consisted of a long corridor of doorways, dimly illuminated by sooty bracket lamps. Finding himself alone in the hallway, Ki listened intently, pressing his ear to each of the closed doors in turn, but heard nothing to indicate that the rooms beyond were occupied, much less by the bearded man. He went back downstairs to the saloon, looking for ways into any back storerooms or such. But there was no rear exit, only a door behind the bar, which ran along the left side of the saloon.

Also behind the bar were two burly bartenders in once-white aprons, and a third man whom Ki assumed was the Antler Inn's proprietor, J. J. Madigan. Short and pudgy, in gray suit trousers and shirtsleeves, the man looked fortyish, with a clipped mustache accentuating the roundness of his face, his dark hair pomaded across a thinning spot, and his black eyes ebullient as he toured the backbar. But whether the man was Madigan or not, neither he nor the bartenders appeared to be in any mood to let Ki through the door without a fuss.

Leaving, Ki went to the left corner of the building and hastened along the side toward the rear. About three-quarters of the way back he came upon a recessed side door, with a tiny stoop and a tinier overhang. There were no other doors, and the few windows were boarded over, and when Ki darted fleetingly to check the saloon's rear, he found that its windows were also planked over.

Moving to the side door, Ki put an ear to its panel, much as he had done upstairs. Hearing nothing, he took a thin, pliant strip of metal from inside his vest, then hunkered down on the stoop and picked the door lock.

Warily he snicked the latch back and pushed the door. Satisfied, he eased inside, closing the door behind him. As his eyes adjusted to the darkness, he found that he was standing in a large pantry. Directly ahead was a double-doored entry to a kitchen, which was unoccupied, though its clutter of foodstuffs and utensils showed that it was in constant use. On his left a long corridor extended to a closed door. Up on the wall beside the door was a bracket lamp, its low flame supplying the corridor's only illumination.

Gently he slid shut the double doors and padded noise-lessly up the dimly lit corridor. He made it even dimmer, reaching out and turning lower the wick of the bracket lamp, then flattened himself against the closed door. He caught the muffled uproar from the saloon area—but he'd even heard that noise while still outside.

This door was unlocked. Gradually Ki cracked the door ajar until it was wide enough for him to slip through, into a windowless room smelling of liquor and cigar smoke. By the bright glow of a parlor lamp suspended from the ceiling, Ki saw that what he'd sneaked into was an office—

no doubt of J. J. Madigan. Along the inner wall was the door that opened out behind the bar, and in the middle of the front wall was an archway leading to an adjacent room, also lamplit, which appeared to be Madigan's living quarters.

At this point Ki considered quietly departing before he was discovered. After all, the bearded man was not here, obviously, and there was nothing to connect the man with Madigan. Nothing, that is, other than one minor detail. Centered in the office was a massive flat desk of mahogany, and on the desk amongst other things was a ship-in-a-bottle. The ship, Ki saw upon closer inspection, was a model of the *Ikatan Queen*. Not only did it resemble Boone Vermillion's steamer, but its name was etched in a little brass plate on the front of the bottle stand.

It didn't prove anything, of course.

But it raised one helluva suspicious odor.

Facing the desk were three hardbacked chairs, and a squat safe that Ki ignored as soon as he discovered it was locked. Behind the desk was a wall of filing cabinets and bookshelves, which, like the desktop and drawers, were crammed with papers. He forged through the litter, rifling the desk, files, and shelves; searching through binders and odd stacks of ledgers; examining documents, accounts, and records. He even rummaged in the wastebasket. He missed little but found little, other than some decks of shaved playing cards and sets of loaded dice.

Next Ki combed the adjacent room. Besides the brass bed, there was a carved oak dresser and wardrobe set, and a commode fashioned like a chair, with a lid over its seat. The usual washbasin and pitcher stood on the dresser, along with a man's leather toilet outfit, and in the dresser were shirts and socks and flannel underwear. A few suits hung in the wardrobe, with discarded clothing shoved in a corner.

The jackpot, Ki concluded disgustedly, was a bust.

He was leaving the bedroom when he heard talking outside the saloon door, the voices garbled by the door and general blare. He moved back to the bedroom as someone began fumbling with the doorknob, and slipped inside the wardrobe, among the suits and dumped clothes. While he was easing the door closed, the saloon door opened.

From the slit in the loosely closed wardrobe doors, Ki could see only a small portion of the office near the saloon door. He glimpsed three men entering—one of the bartenders, the man he assumed was J. J. Madigan, and the bearded man he'd been searching for.

The bearded man seemed all in a huff and puff and was saying: "She was there, aw'ri', just like the hostler reported when he ran in here like his asshole was afire . . ." The men passed from view, then, and the noise from the saloon drowned out their talk, until the man Ki assumed was Madigan yelled: "Shut that damned door, Leroy!" and the bartender reappeared for a moment as he closed the saloon door. Again the talk became clear, Madigan in a querulous tone saying, "This could be serious, Unruh, but it don't sound logical."

"All I know, J. J., is what I tol' you afore," replied the voice of the bearded man. "That Starbuck bitch and her wigwog had their eye on me in the Victoria, but I didn't let on that I cottoned to 'em. They must be up to somethin' agin us, else why was the bitch nosing around about me? Judas, what a spitfire! Wearin' reg'lar man-style duds and totin' a Colt and everythin'. Well, I de-fanged her." There was the clunk of a pistol hitting the desktop. "I didn't check her over real careful-like, though. I mean, p'raps she's got a li'l stingy-gun hid between her udders."

"If there's to be any patting-down done, Unruh, I'll do it," Madigan snapped and a chair squeaked; Ki guessed the proprietor was sitting down at his desk. "Leroy, I think you better go watch her."

"Don't worry, Fowles is with her," Unruh said.

Madigan retorted, "Fowles don't row with both oars. And I ain't sending you back to sit on her, on account you're gonna be busy arrangin' the raid." There was the sound of a match striking, some heavy inhaling, and the smell of a cheap cigar came wafting back to Ki. Madigan continued: "Remember, your job is to sink the *Snohomish*, to once and f'all scuttle that tub to the bottom of the harbor. If Errol Laird chances to die, I ain't gonna weep, but you ain't gonna be paid no bounty for him, either."

"Aw, c'mon, he oughta be worth something dead!"

"Not to Boone Vermillion. Mayhem is one thing, especially when the evidence is underwater, but the law gets finicky about bald murder. Besides, the Lairds turned over Oceana to the Starbuck outfit, so doin' away with Capt'n Errol don't help none. Without a ship, though, Oceana is doomed. And Vermillion doubts that by herself Miss Jessie would have the heart to resist selling out on his terms."

"Okay, it fits," Unruh allowed. "I guess."

"So you ride up to the camp and get the gang. They've been goin' stir-crazy up there, and the exercise will do 'em good. It'll be a pushover. Leroy, didn't I tell you to hang up your apron and git?"

"Yessir!" Again Ki caught sight of Leroy as the bartender stepped to open the saloon door. Behind Leroy came the bearded man—until Madigan snapped, "The other door, Unruh. Take the back hall."

As the saloon door shut on the departing bartender, Unruh turned around and frowned at Madigan. "Why? I was just gonna get a drink afore I left."

"That's why. I don't want no screwups, and you know how you get when you start drinkin'. There'll be a bottle waitin' for you here after the job, but you keep dry till then."

"The hell! I won't—"

"You *will*," Madigan cut in, his chair squeaking as if he were rising. "You'll stay clear of the bar area and go out the back way. Understand?"

Unruh moved toward the desk, out of Ki's sight, but said nothing.

"Understand?" Madigan repeated.

"Yeah."

"Fine. Now, I want to freshen up and think about Miz Starbuck some more, and then I'll collect a couple of the boys out front and go a-calling. I'll wring the truth out of her, and maybe a bill of sale for Oceana, too."

Inside the wardrobe Ki heard Unruh angle toward the hall door. Abruptly, then, he spotted Madigan entering through the archway and stride hastily to the commode. Ki crouched motionless as Madigan, his back to the wardrobe, one-handedly opened his trouser fly while with the other hand he lifted the seat lid. The hall door banged. Madigan, head bent to watch his aim, sighed as he began urinating noisily into the commode's hidden chamber pot.

And Ki sprang out of the wardrobe.

He crossed the small room in three hushed steps. Madigan had time for a distracted "Unruh?" before Ki landed behind him, the calloused edges of both hands axing into either side of Madigan's exposed neck.

Madigan's head snapped forward, the crown of his skull cracking the back panel of the commode. The commode tilted, and he tripped on the suddenly exposed chamber pot. The whole works toppled on its side, the commode

67

fracturing, the chamber pot spilling, and Madigan sprawling limply, never stirring but still unconsciously pissing.

Before Madigan hit the floor, Ki was racing out into the office. He paused only an instant at the desk to scoop up Jessie's revolver, which Unruh had left there, and then dashed for the hall door. He knew what he had to do—he had to catch up with Leroy and trail the bartender to Jessie—and he glanced at the saloon door, tempted to go out that way. But this wasn't mere escape; he must escape unnoticed, before Madigan awoke from his unintentional wet nap and alerted his men. And to succeed, his odds were better against one person than they were against a whole crowded saloon. Even so, it would be difficult to avoid being spotted by Unruh. His only chance was that Unruh was still in the hallway, walking away from Madigan's quarters. In less time than it took to consider this, Ki was at the hall door.

Snaking the latch open, Ki quietly swung the door just enough to slide by, while swiftly reaching around to palm the other knob. He turned as he squeezed through, so that while clearing the door he was also closing it, one hand behind him controlling the knob, the other stretching high to extinguish the hall bracket lamp.

In that instant Ki grinned thinly in relief as he glimpsed Unruh muttering sourly to himself, sauntering a distance ahead but still some yards from the outside door. Then Ki smothered the lamp, pinching the wick of its faint-burning flame, and the corridor was plunged into a darkness as black as the inside of a cave.

"What the fuck!"

Ki eased forward on cat feet. "Unruh," he called in a near whisper, risking a poor imitation of Madigan's voice to draw the gunman.

"J. J., is that you? Mist' Madigan?"

68

Ki thought he could hear Unruh fumbling his way along, and the clunk of a drawn revolver striking the wallboards.

"Hey, J. J.? Get a lamp, why don'tcha?"

Guided by Unruh's voice, Ki approached with swift, light steps on the balls of his feet. He was cocking his arms in a stiff-handed fighter's stance when he bumped blindly into Unruh, but having expected this might happen, he was prepared and slashed his left hand in a chop at the bearded man's neck.

Unruh was not caught napping, however. He brought up his knee to Ki's groin, then they were both spilling to the hallway floor, rolling over and over. Ki had a momentary impression of the man's frenzied haste to wrench free, then felt a blur of gunmetal as Unruh swung the revolver he was gripping. Ki ducked, too late to evade the impact, the gun barrel clouting him along the side of the head, and Unruh scrambled to his feet, thumbing back the gun hammer for a point-blank shot. Ki lunged up and forward, his shoulders hitting Unruh in the gut with a force that carried the man off his feet. The revolver discharged, shooting wild, then clattered against the wall and fell to the floor.

There was no time to grope for the fallen gun. Gaining his footing, Ki heard the whisper of steel against leather as Unruh drew a knife out of a belt sheath. He deflected the stabbing thrust with his forearm and drove a stiff-fingered right hand into the man. But stunned by the gun blast in his face, and staggered from the blow to his head, Ki landed his punch slight off-kilter, cracking a rib low on the man's chest.

Unruh grunted, half lunging, half folding forward. It left him unbalanced for an instant, the sort of opening Ki had been hoping for. He stamped one foot, a little trick

69

to ensure that the foot stayed planted, flat, and immovable. And with his stamp, he snapped his other foot in a side-thrust kick with savage precision, his foot sinking deep in Unruh's abdomen. Lungs emptying of air with a hoarse *whoosh*, Unruh straightened in an arc to the right, then kept on curving over to the floor, where he stayed.

Feeling his way along the corridor wall Ki groped toward the pantry. He fumbled open the outside door, then retraced his steps along the side of the building to the street. Nobody had seen him to recognize him, he felt sure. Even bellied up close and facing Unruh, identification had been impossible in that black abyss. He wondered just how Unruh and Madigan would iron out their suspicions and arguments. Each of them apparently had reason to wonder about the other, perhaps even fear a double-cross, there being no honor among such thieves.

★

# Chapter 6

Trailing Leroy was easy.

Ki caught sight of the bartender not far down the street, striding rapidly without checking to the right, left, or behind him. In his eagerness to obey Madigan's orders, he even refused to veer from the traffic, and the rearing horses and outraged curses in his wake left a spoor that Ki could have followed blindfolded. By the time Leroy reached the bottom of the street, Ki had already figured more or less where he was being led. He paused at the end of the boardwalk while Leroy hastened along the open expanse toward the lumber mill, and when it became clear that Leroy was heading directly for a side door in the main mill building, Ki went after him.

Noiselessly sprinting, Ki rushed straight toward Leroy. If he'd overheard Unruh correctly, another lummox named Fowles was guarding Jessie, and that meant he was going to have to take out both men before Madigan caught up with reinforcements. He could do it more quickly and

71

quietly if he took them out individually. And more safely, too; he didn't want to endanger Jessie any more than necessary.

So, plainly, Ki's aim right then was to stop Leroy, before Leroy could enter the mill.

Leroy was nearly to the side door, his back to Ki and apparently still oblivious to anything other than obeying orders. Ki was closing to within a few yards, running silently on his rope-soled cotton slippers, when he saw Leroy hesitate and heard him mutter, "Now, did Unruh say it was this entrance or the one around t'uther side?" And turning to glance in the direction of this other entrance, Leroy caught peripherally a glimpse of Ki bearing down on him.

"Crap!" he blurted. He was fast. Even as he was shouting, he was pivoting into a crouch, drawing and cocking his revolver in one fluid motion. "Fowles! Fowles!"

Ki threw himself down, twisting his lithe body into a low-rolling somersault. Leroy fired, just as a ferret-faced man wrenched open the door and triggered his pistol, ignoring the risk of hitting Leroy instead of Ki. Lead sizzled inches above Ki, Leroy's revolver so close that it lanced flame in his eyes and singed his left cheek with powder burns.

Yet this was a trifling discomfort compared to the hellish agony Leroy felt an instant later. For Ki, coming out of his roll virtually in front of the bartender, hit him with an uppercutting *nakadaka-ippon-ken* blow, the extended large dexter knuckle of his fist punching Leroy brutally in the crotch, the swift force of his straightening body adding extra power to his swinging jab.

Howling, Leroy sagged to his knees, forgetting his revolver and letting it drop, while he cupped his groin in both hands. Ki, sidestepping, knowing Leroy was effectively through for this fight, dived for the other man. Fowles gaped mystified at Leroy, who, after a moment of writhing and shrieking, lapsed into unconsciousness.

That moment allowed Fowles to recover; face gnarling with rage, he aimed his pistol at Ki. Ki launched into a *tobi-geri* flying kick, sailing into the doorway and striking Fowles in the chest with his extended left foot. His ferocious spring buckled Fowles, carrying him backward into the lumber mill, the pistol firing with a deafening roar alongside Ki's ear. Fowles smashed hard against a pile of crates, but he remained upright, leveling his .45.

Ki swiveled away from the doorway. Fowles was thumbing the hammer of his single-action Colt when Ki snatched up a wagon stay chain from a bunch that were draped over a spare harness rig. He lashed out with it, the twenty-six inches of twisted links snaking around Fowles's head and whipping across his eyes. Again his pistol discharged, and again the bullet whispered by Ki's ear as it sped harmlessly outside.

The shot was still reverberating when Ki, pulling savagely on the chain, jerked Fowles stumbling toward him. He halted Fowles with a *yonhon nukite*, the spearheading tips of his stiffened fingers knifing into Fowles's throat and rupturing his trachea. With a raspy sigh Fowles wilted and died.

"Thank God," Jessie said, tremulous with relief.

"Thank Him after we get out of here," Ki replied, unsheathing a knife as he crossed to where Jessie was tied to the post. "We're due for company any minute now. Company you don't want to keep."

"That whiskery brute, Unruh?"

"No, his boss. Or rather, one of his bosses," Ki said, then related what he'd encountered at the Antler Inn while

73

he continued slicing through the tough leather belting. When he'd finished and Jessie was freed, he concluded by saying: "What's still unclear to me is whether J. J. Madigan is partners with Boone Vermillion, or a kind of local lieutenant of his, or just subcontracting the dirty work here for him."

"Well, whatever his arrangement with Vermillion, Madigan seems to have a gang stashed at some camp. Up in the hills, by the sound of it. I'd say our main problem now is to stop them raiding the *Snohomish*." Jessie rubbed her wrists thoughtfully, then took her pistol, which Ki had brought along from Madigan's office. "Maybe you've already squelched the raid, Ki. Did you kill Unruh?"

"I didn't stay to check. I hope not."

They were heading for the doorway as Ki spoke. But reaching it, in that instant before actually stepping outside, they spotted Madigan and four gunmen—who simultaneously spotted them. Three of the gunmen were hunkering quizzically around the comatose Leroy, and at this moment Madigan and the fourth man were straightening and walking toward the door.

Jessie sprang to grab the door, only to find that Fowles's body was in the way, preventing her from slamming it shut. While Ki, backing, scooped up Fowles's fallen revolver with such speed that his movement was a blur.

But Madigan reacted with equal swiftness. He dug a snubnosed .32 "hammerless" pocket pistol out of a shoulder holster, beating even the draw of the man beside him, who cleared leather with an S&W .44. Yet it was the gunman who excitedly yelled, "I got 'em, I got 'em!" and was the first to trigger, with more haste than sense.

His .44 slug sang past Ki and buried itself in the post where Jessie had been tied. Then the gunman's right arm

74

flopped limply, the gun dropping from nerveless fingers as Ki's answering blast drilled a blood-spurting hole through his shoulder. The man reeled dizzily, while behind him the other three now leapt to action, one pointing a revolver and the other two leveling sawed-off shotguns. Momentarily their shots were blocked by Madigan and the wounded man, and before they could spread and catch the doorway in a crossfire, Ki sent them scattering by creasing one in the thigh.

"Kill them!" Madigan was ranting, waving rather than firing his nickel-plated pistol. Warily the three began to regroup in a shifting line. The wounded gunnie picked up his pistol, gritting his teeth as he lifted his revolver in his left hand to try again.

Jessie had been struggling to drag Leroy's body away from the door, all the while wanting to scream at Ki to get back, to get down, to stop setting himself up as a target to draw their fire. She knew that was what he was doing for her, just as she knew that he was carefully nursing the pitifully few bullets in Leroy's revolver. It was a horrifying sacrifice for Ki or anyone to make, and partly in desperation, partly in defiance, Jessie now dropped Leroy's legs and joined Ki by the doorway, bringing her pistol to bear.

"No—" Ki started to protest as Jessie, feeling no compunction, shot the wounded gunman in his left chest. The man teetered, bumping against Madigan before falling sidelong at the saloon owner's feet.

Off-balance and windmilling his arms, Madigan tripped on the gunman's carcass as he backed up. "Kill 'em, you idjits!" he wailed as he toppled ungainly over him, sprawling flat on his back, unaware that Jessie's second bullet had just passed through the space where his navel had been. "Kill 'em!"

Reholstering her pistol, Jessie frantically returned to rolling Leroy aside. With crows of delight both shotgunners cut loose just as, together, Jessie and Ki slammed the door and dropped the dead bolt. The shotguns' twelve-gauge rounds rattled the door and kicked up a storm of splinters from its facing, but none of the buck passed through.

But the next hit might. The shotguns could—and eventually would—pulverize the door, and Jessie and Ki knew that their breathing spell could be counted in seconds. The windows were too high and too small to squeeze through and would only land them back in the gunmen's midst. Their only prayer of escape was out the back and through the mill.

Grasping Jessie's hand, Ki started running through the narrow passages between the stockpiled equipment. Behind them they could hear Madigan's raving, the throaty discharge of shotguns, and the rending crack of door panels. Turning, Ki saw a hand worming through a hole gouged in the wood, straining to lift the latch. Aiming carefully, he spent a bullet to smash the hand, which was hastily withdrawn with a muffled shriek of pain.

They raced on, the accumulated stores gradually lessening, the aisles widening, until they came to another door built into a partition wall. It had no lock but was barred on this side with a stout piece of lumber wedged in iron brackets. Ki yanked out the wooden crossbar, flinging it aside and prying open the door as the storeroom reverberated with the volleys of buckshot demolishing the side door behind.

"Goddammit, fools, hustle!" came Madigan's echoing voice, his men finally gaining entry. "You're letting them get away through the mill!"

Jessie and Ki surged into a long, open section of the mill filled with raw logs awaiting cutting. Ahead of them stretched a row of long platforms with rollers and blocking boards, along which the logs would be directed to chutes, which led in turn to huge circular saw blades farther on. The whole kaboodle was operated by an interconnected series of pulleys, shafts, and leather-strap belts and was no doubt powered by a steam engine somewhere nearby.

As they dashed past the murk-shrouded platforms and chutes, Ki glimpsed the dark silhouette of a conveyor belt sloping up through a boarded-in structure to another part of the mill. Because the conveyor started down near the sawblades, he guessed it was used to haul the bark, kindling, and other leftovers when the logs were sawed into lumber. If so, then it would lead to an incinerator outside the building, where the trash wood would be burned. He was about to forget it, to seek an easier exit, when he heard Madigan's voice call out: "Edgar, cover that door over there! It's the only other way out of this section. We've got 'em boxed in, boys, they're trapped!"

Again Ki clutched Jessie's hand, this time making her veer with him toward the conveyor. Scrambling over its low, galvanized iron sides, they began climbing the broad yet steeply inclined belting, puncturing their hands with slivers on the scraps of raw-cut wood debris.

"Hey, J. J., they ain't here! You think they could be up that there conveyor? Yeah, I sees 'em! There they are!"

The thin metal siding of the conveyor shook, and chunks of plankboard wall cascaded around Jessie and Ki as, ducking, they felt volleys of twelve-gauge buck rocketing around them. Desperately, with sweat rivuleting and muscles aching, they kept on with their scrambling

77

climb. At last they reached the uppermost point, where the conveyor fed into another conveyor that led more or less horizontally out of the building. Here there was a small landing and a catwalk that flanked the second conveyor to a hatchway in the outside wall. They hurried along the catwalk to the hatch, the mill below them resonating with the infuriated shouts and curses of Madigan and his men swarming to intercept them.

The hatch opened out onto another catwalk, this one running high along the outside of the building. The conveyor angled off across a trestle of sorts to an incinerator perched near the river; the incinerator resembled a giant sheet-iron-sided tepee, as tall as the building, capped by a domed screen to serve as a smoke flue and spark arrestor. Figuring that to take the conveyor would only trap them atop the incinerator, Jessie and Ki scurried along the catwalk, searching for stairs—only to see that one of the gunmen had beaten them and was climbing the steps two at a time. Ki aimed at him, unsure whether the late Leroy had worn his revolver smart, with an empty chamber under its hammer, or stupid, with a sixth and now final round ready to fire.

But the man coming up didn't know about Ki's gamble, and he wouldn't have covered Ki's bet if he had. The mere sight of the muzzle's dead-on maw was so unnerving that after rearing back in panic, spasmodically triggering his shotgun and fountaining buckshot straight up into the air, the man turned tail and fled, yelling, back down the stairs.

Before the stumbling gunman had reached bottom, Jessie and Ki were moving around the next corner of the catwalk. They spied the roof of a shed below, projecting from the side of the building. The shed was apparently protecting the steam engine that powered the mill's machinery and,

78

like a huge stepping-stone, stuck out midway between the catwalk and the ground. Still, it was a fair drop, and the roof looked weak.

Yet Madigan and company were charging both ways, up the stairs and out the hatch by the conveyor. "*Now* we got 'em!"

Jessie hitched her legs over the catwalk railing and let herself fall, followed by Ki. They struck the tar-papered roof, the boards underneath them wobbling and splintering but managing not to break. Wreathed in pluming sawdust, they clambered across the springy roof to its edge and jumped to the ground, stirring up another geyser of dust and grit.

"Goddammit, they're down there!" Madigan shouted in rage, leaning over the railing above. "Don't stand here! Edgar, after 'em!"

The shotgunner named Edgar, his eyes watering from the dust, promptly dived for the shed. At the same instant Ki wheeled and squeezed the trigger. Leroy had been stupid. His revolver's last bullet bored high into Madigan's left arm, upending him again, and simultanously rattling Edgar as he fell. While the other men poured curses and gunfire from the ledge, Edgar landed off-balance. Ripping tar paper and cracking boards, he plummeted into the shed with a horrendous crash, more layers of suddenly disturbed dust erupting out through the hole he'd made.

Jessie and Ki plunged around the edge of the mill building, Ki tossing the useless revolver far away. As one proud of his marksmanship, it galled him to have merely winged Madigan, and he thought disgustedly that the gunbarrel might have a curve to it—perhaps due to Leroy having bent it over some victim's skull.

"Get your hands off me!" Madigan could be heard bawling. "You imbecile, that's where I'm wounded! Never mind me, get after those two. Get to the stairs, the stairs, quick!"

The gunmen on the ledge made a trampling dash for the steps, but the sounds of their pursuit faded as Jessie and Ki tore across the mill yard. Heading across the open stretch, they sprinted back into town. Realizing that the main street would offer little concealment from the gunmen chasing after them, they cut across it and slipped into the alley by the hardware store, pausing in its shadows to catch their breath.

"We can't rest here," Ki panted. "They'll be breaking the town apart, looking for us, and Madigan's probably got more men he'll be calling on to help."

"The *Snohomish*." Jessie leaned her hand against the wall to steady herself, still quivering from exertion. "Got to warn Errol about the raid."

"Then what?"

"Why, get set for the raid, of course."

"How?" Ki pressed and began ticking off reasons on his fingers. "First, we don't know when the raid will come. Second, if we did, they could change the time to catch us off-guard. Third, Laird doesn't have enough crew to act as guards and still repair his ship. Fourth, even if he did have them, who knows how many aren't ringers like Tabac, who'll betray the ship if they're put on guard duty. And fifth, Madigan's no dummy. He's probably already sent men to watch for us at the harbor."

Jessie mulled for a moment, then: "Now I catch why you hoped you hadn't killed Unruh. If he's dead, Madigan will just put someone else in charge of the raid—someone we don't know and can't track."

"Uh-huh. And the only way to stop the raid is to stop the gang—or at least to learn of their plans—and that means trailing Unruh to their camp."

"Meaning we head for the livery and ride out," Jessie reckoned, and by the glint in her eye, she wasn't entirely displeased with the notion of meeting the treacherous hostler again.

In a slight crouch they hurried on up behind the line of buildings toward the livery stable. Reaching the rear of the livery without detection, they darted alongside the stable barn to the front and spotted the hostler standing out in the yard. They hunkered a moment, gauging their chances—which appeared slim to none, until the hostler started a few steps down the street, staring in the direction of the lumber mill.

Softly they toed around toward the open stable doors, glimpsing Madigan, clutching his arm, and his gunmen reach the end of the boardwalk and fan out searching. They dipped inside the barn. Quickly, yet as quietly as possible, they located the moro and the sorrel mare, gratified to find that the horses were still saddled, the hostler evidently lazy as well as gabby. They led their mounts out of the stalls and tightened the cinches, hoping to hide whatever noise they were making in the clamor of the hunt, hearing the gunmen calling to one another in the street and alleyways.

Then closer, much closer, they heard: "Who's there?"

They swiveled and crouched against the splintered wheel of a rotting freight wagon, motionless in the dimness as the hostler entered the barn in a sort of gnarled trot. Spying the two horses, he grumbled and spat and moved disgustedly toward them.

"Now, how'd you get loose—"

The hostler ended his question in a choking gargle. Ki, rising behind him as he passed, clamped his left hand over the hostler's mouth and at the same time smashed the rock-hard heel of his right hand squarely between

81

the hostler's eyes. The hostler's teeth clacked together and his head snapped back, whipping his body off his feet. He dropped flat on his back atop a pile of manured hay, where Ki figured he would sleep for the next twelve hours at least.

Jessie vaulted into the saddle. Ki grabbed for the reins, but his feisty moro shied away, and his foot missed the stirrups the first couple of tries. Their horses champed at their bits, wanting to be run, but neither Jessie nor Ki had any idea of what to expect outside, where Madigan and his men were, or how many guns would respond if they were detected. So they chose to take a quiet gait that would be less likely to attract attention.

Nerves screwed tight, they passed around the back of the livery and continued up along the rear of the town. Naturally they were aware that their efforts could be all for nothing. There was no guarantee that Unruh was alive, or had left for the gang, or had even gone in this direction— and they were not about to go around front of the Antler Inn to see if his grulla was still there. On the other hand, assuming the gang was camped up in the hills, the only route heading east into the mountainous coastal range was the wagon road that began at the upper end of the main street. And so far they had not heard Unruh among the growing contingent of gunmen joining Madigan. Unruh's state of health was still unknown, but this would all be resolved once they were clear of Port Tenino, and Ki could check the wagon road for tracks of the grulla. That was the chief *if*—getting safely out of town.

They had almost come to the last set of structures when Ki caught the sudden pounding of boots from somewhere not far behind. He jumped his moro sideward, grabbing Jessie's horse by the bit to keep from losing her, and plunged into the shadows of a narrow alleyway between two buildings. There they pulled up, waiting.

Less than a minute later a pair of gunmen hustled by them, almost at arm's reach.

"Fast workers," Ki murmured as the footfalls receded streetward. He nudged his horse moving again and brought them out behind the rear of the buildings again. More swiftly now, they threaded among the final cluster of cabins and hovels. At last they cleared Port Tenino proper but kept to the cover of flanking trees, boulders, and scrub for quite some distance before easing onto the wagon road. From behind them, out of sight, came faint shouts and hoofbeats, the sounds radiating high and echoing off of the tree-clad slopes ahead of them.

After a stretch they cut from the road to a spindly wedge of trees and reined in to allow their horses a breather. Walking to the road, Ki began searching for tracks in the bed, and not surprisingly he found plenty. He shifted a short distance away to survey their general layout, then crisscrossed to sort out and piece together who had gone where with what. Shortly he found the mark of the grulla's telltale shoe.

The print gave them a heartening boost.

They continued easterly along the road's sinuously twisting route, with a partially overcast sky developing above, and stony outcroppings and tall-wooded flanks encroaching on all sides. Along about midafternoon they came to a fork which wound southerly. Again Ki dismounted, carefully checking to see which way Unruh had ridden his grulla. This time Unruh had gone on along the wagon road, but three miles later tracks showed he had cut off onto a side trail. That in due course led to other paths at branches and crossings, yet all were deeply rutted and ascended roughly eastward through rock outcrops and thick groves.

Presently Jessie and Ki began twining in and out of steepening culverts and ridge-flanking woods, flexing toward an increasingly tumbled upland of staggered slopes, creek-bottom gulches, and dense stands of timber. At one intersection of trails, where a rivulet formed a patch of soggy ground, they noticed a morass of recently churned horse prints joining in from the other trail, out of the north, and they continued on ahead to a dry flinty rise upon which hooves left no sign at all.

"The gang?" Jessie wondered aloud.

The route was marked by indigo and burgundy shadows when they came to a broad knoll. Here the trail abruptly split, one fork wandering away from the knoll, the other advancing straight toward a hill of rock. There were no obvious hoofprints along either fork, so they reined in to scout about, only to find their attention diverted by the rock. A half-mile off amid low spurs and ledges, the rock soared about two hundred feet high by three hundred around, towering like an eroded, fissured monument, giving the impression it could topple any time. Despite its appeal, though, Ki soon detected a fresh white score on a stone slab—the kind of scrape made by the iron of a shod horse.

Jessie pointed at the rock. "To there?"

Ki nodded. "Unruh may be close as the other side of the rock, but even if not, we just keep on that trail fork, we'll come to him."

"We'll come to the gang, you mean. Surely they must've posted sentries to watch their backup and trail, and they've only to hear us, and we'll reap a hot welcome. We're going to have to get there from an unexpected direction." She gestured at the other fork. "Where's it go? Do you think it skirts the rock?"

"Let's find out," Ki said, and nosed his moro forward.

They turned onto this lesser trail, constantly surveying the terrain ahead, on both sides, and behind. Soon heavy brush flanked the trail, obscuring details, though with the rock hill as a landmark, it was apparent the trail was hooking at an angle around the far end of the hill. As they approached the hill on this curve, boulders and large stone slabs crowded the trail, until finally they came to a little open glade, with the rock looming near on their right. The sun had set by now, and evening was fast encroaching.

"Looks about close as we'll get on horseback," Jessie allowed.

Quietly they dismounted. Single file they led their mounts up a gentle slope, and after Jessie took a box of ammunition from her saddlebag, they climbed on foot toward an aspen-crowned ridge. At the crest they ground-reined their horses and glided hunching to the other side of the ridge, where they knelt down in the concealing brush and stared down into a canyon below.

The canyon was compact, its sides gentle and profuse with brier, thickets, boulders, and copses—except for the side formed by the rock, a grizzled slab ending in a barren shale-slide embankment. At the top of the slanting embankment was the dark maw of a cave, although the mouth appeared to be supported by timbers, like the entrance to a mine. Through the center of the canyon rippled a stream, and between the stream and the embankment was a group of crude log buildings: bunkhouses, a cookshack and mess hall, a cache house, a wagon shed, and a corraled stable. On the other side of the stream they could see a small mill and drying sheds outlined dimly in the dusky twilight.

"Well, I'll be damned," Ki whispered. "A logging camp."

Lamps burned in a couple of the bunkhouses and the mess hall, and a billow of sparks was rising from the cookshack stovepipe. There was no sign of Unruh or anyone else about the buildings or farther out in the canyon.

"What a break," Jessie murmured. "It must be chow time, and they're all in the mess hall. Well, while they're all in there, let's take a quick gander through the hall's rear window, there. I want to know if Unruh is here."

Creeping silently, careful not to dislodge a loose stone or snap a brittle twig, they stole down the slope and across to within twenty yards of the mess hall's rear. The remaining distance was all open ground, though. They angled toward the blind side of a bunkhouse that ran the way they wanted to go and would favor them with a much shorter stretch of exposure. They advanced along the wall of the bunkhouse, under the shadow of the eaves, almost crawling by the time they reached the corner.

A man—a late diner, apparently—swept around the corner and collided with Ki. He was startled but rebounded instantly and drew. He also had a quick-draw holster, which practically fed the butt of his revolver into his palm if he so much as flicked his wrist.

He fired twice, but the second shot was pure reflex; he was already dead. Both shots sailed off harmlessly into the sky as he went over backward with the handle of Ki's *tanto* protruding from the loose flesh beneath his chin. Ki had been just a bit faster, stepping forward just as the man drew, bringing the point of the knife upward with savage force, plunging the blade through muscle, tendon, and bone, and into the man's brain stem. As the man hit the ground on his back, Ki moved in. Placing a foot on the man's face for leverage, he pulled out the blade. Jessie winced and turned away.

"I guess that blows it," Ki said as from inside the mess hall arose a confusion of voices and a clatter of running footsteps. Immediately Jessie and Ki started at a run for the nearest place they could make a stand—the cave entrance.

They reached the last of the log cabins, and put it between them and their pursuers. Then, lunging up the sloping rockslide, they made a third of the distance before the first shot came. It clipped Jessie's sleeve, and she shied, looking back over her shoulder, only to trip and sprawl forward, clutching her pistol to keep it from being knocked loose. The fall saved her life, for a veritable hail of gunfire swept above them as Ki also dropped to hug the rocks.

On hands and knees Jessie swiveled around and triggered her pistol. A thin yell drifted up at her, and the men paused in their firing. She got to her feet and, with Ki alongside, raced up the grade in a low-crouching scramble toward the shelter of the cave. More rifle and pistol fire chased them now, splintering the thick support beams at the entrance and whining deep into the tunnel beyond as they plunged inside.

"I'll check, you cover!" Ki shouted, and before Jessie could answer, he had sprinted past, cat-footed, to see who or what was in back.

She pivoted and bellied down on the entrance floor, sighting her revolver. Below, a half-dozen men with drawn guns were charging up the slope toward the cave. Behind them swarmed others, one of whom snapped up his rifle and fired a chance shot. It came close, the lead whispering by her ear.

Then she began to fire, feeling the recoil in her arm with each shot, hearing the metallic clack of the hammer when the pistol finally emptied. Hastily reloading, she measured her dwindling shots, forcing the gunmen to dive for shelter, stalling their attack. One lay in the open and did not move. Jessie aimed again, and another of Madigan's gang failed to reach shelter. She swung the barrel and targeted the body of a man leaping for the embankment. She fired, and the man moved three more staggering steps forward before collapsing on his face and lying still.

Answering lead began to reach for her as the gang riddled the cave mouth with volley after volley. From his shelter behind the nearest cabin, one of them shouted orders to some of the others. A jabbering reply that sounded like agreement came from one of the others, and four of them hastened to one of the sheds beyond the bunkhouses. When they reappeared, each carried a partially filled gunnysack, and then, splitting into pairs, they began to dash for the base of the rockslide at opposite ends. Despite his bandaged face and puffy, mottled eyes, the one who had first shouted orders was immediately recognizable as Unruh.

The rest of the gunmen broke out with a renewed concentration of fire, while Jessie trained on Unruh and the other three, triggering and reloading, counting her rapidly depleting bullets. Ki returned from his reconnaissance of the cave and slewed in beside her, saying, "Nothing back there, and no way out!"

"Those two pair, coming from either side! One's Unruh, and I bet anything he's got them carrying black powder in those bags!" As she spoke, Jessie fired twice more. One of the four fell over his gunnysack. "If any of them gets to the cliff, he'll be out of our range, and one can of powder tossed in here . . ."

She left the obvious unspoken, pressing the trigger once more. The firing pin again came down on an empty chamber. Once more she reloaded, then downed another man. A third stumbled but kept crawling, until Jessie blew his brains out.

And Unruh reached the top of the slide. The gang below cheered him on, pouring raking gunfire into the cave entrance. Jessie moved to the best possible point from which to shoot, ignoring the searing ricochets as she tried to pick off Unruh. But her efforts were not enough. Pressed flat against the cliff face, Unruh could advance stealthily toward the mouth of the cave without fear that she'd be able to hit him except by stepping outside, which would be sheer suicide.

"We'll have to fall back!" Jessie cried.

Ki shook his head. "It'd be a waste of time. Besides, we may have a chance, if Unruh didn't think to bring a rope."

"A rope! I'm not worried about any rope! The powder—"

"And how is he going to chuck it in here? With a rope, unless he wasn't smart enough to bring one, and then he'll throw by hand."

Before Jessie could ask more, Ki squirreled across to the far side. Easing upright, pressing flat against the cave wall, he tried to become as thin as possible to avoid the barrage of bullets bracketing the entrance.

Then, as if to answer Jessie, the firing tapered off. And she realized that Unruh must not have a rope; he'd have to get within throwing range, and they'd have to slack off or hit him. And Ki—

Ki was gone. Before the last bullet cracked, he'd launched himself out of the cave. For a split second he was in full view of the gang below, who were expectantly regrouping in a surging mass up the rockslide. He was also glimpsed by Unruh, who was poised in an awkward, one-legged stance to pitch. He faced Ki from all of four feet away, the gunnysack bunched in his belt, a lighted match in one hand, and a canister of black stump-blasting powder in the other, its fuse sputtering and throwing off sparks.

It was his final conscious sensation.

Unruh never did see the blur of Ki's hands as three *shuriken* winked in the moonlit air. He died before the visual message could reach his brain, blood jetting from his heart, right lung, and throat. From below, the gunmen were already unleashing a withering torrent. Lead thudded into timbers and sprayed biting stone fragments around Ki as, the instant the third *shuriken* left his fingertips, he dived back inside the cave. And Unruh, arms vainly clutching his chest, hinged forward with the canister of black powder folded in his death's embrace and rolled down the slope.

Initially the gunmen were so intent upon slaughtering Ki that they didn't pay much attention to Unruh tumbling into their midst. When belatedly they did, even the most courageous of them reeled and began scattering and retreating. The pistol blasts from inside the tunnel mouth ripped into them—

Then the canister exploded. The earth shook, and the gunmen and a large section of the rockslide were swallowed in flame and smoke. After a moment debris began pelting down, including grisly chunks of flesh and bone.

The cave entrance was an inferno. The air turned acrid, and powder fumes strangled their lungs. Strange, invisible hands plucked at their clothing, yet Ki managed to yell through his choking, "Get set, Jessie! They should be charging us any moment now."

But as the billowing clouds dissipated, they saw that the surviving gang members were breaking for their horses in the corral. The toll was too great; it had been too large already, but this black powder disaster was more than they were being paid to buck. The slope and canyon floor were dotted with dead and dying gunmen. Those who turned and fled had to leap clear of the carnage.

"Sort of fitting," Jessie said when things grew quiet. "The rats were caught in their own trap. They're leaving the ship instead of sinking one."

Ki stared down, then gazed at the night sky before turning to her. "Let's get going, too. This place makes me sick."

Returning to Port Tenino, they found the town quiet except for some rowdy saloon patrons. They left their horses off at the livery, where the hostler was still lying unconscious, and boarded the *Snohomish* without incident.

Only to Errol Laird did Jessie confide the day's happenings.

Ki told nothing to nobody.

★

# Chapter 7

Next morning found the Antler Inn padlocked and J. J. Madigan missing. The vagrant gunhands Jessie had noticed before were absent from their posts in front of the saloons, and though the town's abnormal calm provoked much gossip and speculation, Jessie, Ki, and Laird offered no opinions, much less explanations. They were just silently glad that work on the *Snohomish* could continue safely and uneventfully.

Chief Engineer Norris's prediction of a week proved close to the mark. But at the end of six full days, the engine was reassembled, steam was up, and the tired crew chafing to depart. There were no cheers, no crowd of people to see the ship off.

By now word had come through Port Tenino by way of trollers and southbound steamers that salmon were showing off the Southgates, the Deserters group, even up into Johnstone Strait. That meant there was a good chance they were already spawning up the tributaries that fed Glacier Bay. And every day Oceana missed fishing and canning was one day closer to ruination—and nobody could forecast how thick the salmon would run, or for how long before they'd abruptly, mysteriously vanish till next season.

So, even though Madigan's plot to sink the ship had been foiled, the delay for repairs made the odds look bleak for the *Snohomish* to arrive in time to make a success of this season. Only unreasoning stubbornness drove Capt'n Errol and crew toward the only goal that was left for them. Helmsmen rubbed tobacco in their eyes to keep awake. The engines remained wide open and would remain that way day and night till the bitter end. Hands reeled with exhaustion as they stoked the fires, depending on their mates to drag them into bunks. They ate when they could and slept the same way. It was a suicide pace.

Still, the *Snohomish* was eating up the miles and that brought a kind of peace to Jessie and Ki. Ahead lay a tricky, heartless sea that was no respecter of plans, persons, or ships. Ahead lay fuel camps where it took money on the line for wood or coal or other supplies, and practically all the cash on board had gone for repairs. But they were a fighting outfit, ready to battle to the death to reach their goal.

On and on, driving—driving. Spring brought morning fog along the Inland Passage, which sometimes lifted during the day. Sometimes it didn't. The *Snohomish* had to cope with that added hazard, running time-and-compass courses in the murk and guided by blasts from the steam whistle echoing back from the nearby shoreline. Again savage storms flayed the coast. The surf rose and fell, and still the bow of the *Snohomish* breasted the current as the crew fought their hearts out. The strain was telling, though. The hands grew gaunt, snappish, but never once did a man spare himself. Save for fuel stops, the steamer never faltered. Full speed ahead by day and by night.

As the steamer approached Seymour Narrows, the cannery crew came on deck. Here the ship was forced to advance under slow bell, with the caution of something living fearing ambush. Ragged granite fangs awaited unwary hulls. There were swirls and overfalls around Ripple Rock. A floating log vanished, as if it were plucked under by some mighty hand.

The channel narrowed until they were in the shadow of a mountain. On either side the land leapt abruptly from the sea. Spruces grew so close to the water's edge that the salty spray killed the lower branches. The bright green of their massed tops was shot with splashes of silver, the naked trunks of long dead trees stretching twisting arms mutely forth. There was scant soil on some of the sheer ridges, where the snow line was slowly retreating, spilling numberless cascades and waterfalls through the green forest. High above brooded the eternal glaciers and snowfields, clinging precariously to granite peaks.

Jessie caught brief flashes of nameless inlets and coves; of valleys shrouded in mystery. There were moments when the passage seemed like a landlocked lake high in the mountains; when it seemed as if they must surely crash onto the beach, a channel appeared and the way was open. . . . But often as not, fog shrouded the landscape in vapors that blew like eddying billows of smoke. Gray mists pressed in on all sides. At times, above the blasts of the steam whistle and the sounds of the ship plying the sea, Jessie could hear the wing flapping of startled water birds. Land was close—damn close.

When the whistle blast came again, she began counting. One tenth of the elapsed time between whistle's blast and return of the echo was the distance, in nautical miles, that the steamer was from the land that had caused the echo.

"We're about a half mile off shore," Jessie remarked tentatively as she stepped onto the bridge. Capt'n Errol nodded. He was leaning on the bridge rail, staring intently ahead. As the fog thinned momentarily, Jessie saw the bow lookout—a gray ghost of a man, tense and alert. The steamers slowed until there was only a faint trickle around the bows.

Laird cursed under his breath. "Glacier Bay is an ideal location for a salmon cannery," he commented, "but there's a vast ice sheet at the head of the inlet that manufactures fogs on a large scale."

Duncan McArdle appeared, yawning. "Same old stuff, eh?"

When the whistle sounded again, the echo returned in two seconds. It was followed a moment later by a second echo, then two more. McArdle computed their position and announced it.

Laird chuckled. "Maybe you'd like to take the bridge, Duncan?"

"Not me, Cap. I brought a tug and scowload of salmon through here once when the Ol' Boss was sick. It took ten years off'n my life."

Not wishing to distract Laird further, Jessie left the captain to his concerns and returned with McArdle to the boat deck. When the whistle sounded again, its echo almost blended with its blast. Deep within, a gong sounded and water boiled astern. Jessie could hear a pump throbbing in the engine room.

"Backin' up," McArdle whispered to Jessie. "I'll bet Capt'n Errol anchors. He didn't get the echo he wanted. This fog's goin' to hang on. We may be here a week."

Jessie didn't answer, though she had to agree. The engines were going ahead again now. Abruptly they stopped, and Jessie waited expectantly for Laird to order the hook dropped. Instead the engines stirred cautiously, like a man who expected to get shot lifting his head from the the brush.

McArdle grunted. "He's decided to risk going on."

Uncertainty got the upper hand, but rather than go back up to see Laird, Jessie paced back and forth for the better part of an hour. Each time the whistle blasted, she started violently. Suddenly she felt the stern swing starboard. The *Snohomish* fairly crawled for the next fifteen minutes. Water birds continued to get up under the bows, their eerie, alarmed cries drifting back through the fog.

The whistle sounded, and then a curious thing happened. Echoes fairly leapt at them from port and starboard. There was a long delay, then a third echo returned. Jessie held her breath. A crash like thunder filled the air. It trailed into a series of faint booms. Then there was silence. They were squarely between the headlands that marked Glacier Bay.

Laird appeared, shouting orders down to the hands.

"Swell work, Capt'n Errol," McArdle called up. "I thought for sure we would anchor a couple of times."

"Luck," Laird answered, "fisherman's luck. Sometimes fisherman's luck is bad, sometimes good, but in the end it balances."

The steamer moved on into Glacier Bay under slow bell, skirting wallowing bergs and heading, according to Laird, toward the cannery. Someone was hammering a triangle at intervals to mark its location. At last out of the fog heaved a small wharf, jutting out from the wooded shore. Several cannery tenders and barges were moored to the wharf, on which a handful of men in oilskins were now congregating as the ship approached. A line was heaved dockward, where two of the men caught it and hauled in the hawser hand over hand, then dropped it over a mooring post. Two more lines followed, and slowly the heavily laden steamer drifted against the wharf. The gangplank dropped, and one of the men hastened aboard.

"Hello, Capt'n Errol!" he exclaimed. "Where's Ol' Boss?"

"In the hospital, I'm afraid, in a pretty bad way. I'm trying to run the show this season," Laird answered. "Foxclaw, meet Jessica Starbuck and Ki. Jessie, Ki, this's Foxclaw, my cannery superintendent and head of my winter men— the men who stay on here as watchmen when the cannery is closed down."

As Jessie and Ki were later to learn, *Foxclaw* was not the superintendent's real name. It was merely a close approximation of his unpronounceable Indian name, for Foxclaw was a mission-educated member of the local Tlingit tribe. The native Alaskan was grizzled, his legs were bowed, and his hands were knotted with two fingers missing; but his firm brown skin belied his years, and his eyes, peering from beneath badgerlike brows, had the boring faculty of steel drills. At the moment, as he turned back to Errol Laird, he was staring with sadness, though he carried an expression of stout optimism on his seamed face.

"Your dad won't go down without a fight," he told Laird, returning to their conversation. "Here, everything is ready. We've got the boats and barges in the water, and the machinery's been gone over and tested. Some replacements are needed. Here's a list of things that need to be done." He handed Laird several sheets of paper. "We overhauled the floating trap, of course. Whenever you say the word, it's ready to be towed to Manitou Point and moored. A little work needs to be done on the scows.

We figured the crew could do that while we're waiting for the run to start."

They went ashore, giving Jessie and Ki a chance to look around. The cannery buildings, adjacent bunkhouses, and a series of cabins had been erected on a mass of slab rock, the whitewashed structures standing out sharply against the background of emerald green. Just beyond roared a waterfall where a creek broke from the dense timber and reached the bay in a fifty-foot leap, supplying unlimited quantities of clear icy water for the cannery's operations. The rest of the surroundings was shrouded invisible in fog.

The fog lifted three days later, revealing an enchanted region. The bay was long and narrow and had obviously been carved out of the enclosing mountains by a glacier. It was a live glacier, constantly discharging ice, constantly growling and roaring as the mass shifted and tons of ice fell from a face over a mile in width and one hundred feet high. When Jessie and Ki first caught sight of it, sunlight was flashing rare tints of green and blue that broke the blinding white.

Ravens flapped about on black wings and voiced gloomy complaints in harsh voices. A totem pole leered from the center of the Tlingit village, which was situated roughly midway between the glacier and the cannery. Swarthy, bright-eyed youngsters, followed by spirited dogs, played about. Several of the older natives probed a brawny stream with gaff hooks fixed to long poles. Habit is strong, and the creek that had supplied their ancestors with winter's food still served them.

Errol Laird recounted how he'd often seen the creek, and others like it around the bay, so choked with salmon that those below forced the ones above partly out of the water. The spawning runs were smaller now, but still ample, and important to the white men because it heralded the main run off Manitou Point.

Tenders and tugs sent towlines aboard the floating trap several days later, and the unwieldy structure, followed by scows carrying anchors and gear, moved slowly down the bay. Jessie and Ki went along with Laird, and as they neared Manitou Point, they could feel the lift and fall of the sea. The water was too deep for a pile trap. It was at times almost too rough for a floating trap, but the site was one of the best in the north. Salmon swam against the current, and as there was an eddy off Manitou Point, it was possible to trap fish when the tide was both rising and falling.

Scows dropped heavy anchors at the designated angles to keep the trap in position regardless of wind, tide, and weather. Logs two feet in diameter were bolted and braced until they formed a solid frame. Three-inch lead pipes, driven through logs, extended thirty feet into the water. The pipes supported the netting that trapped the salmon. A lead, constructed of logs, pipes, and netting, extended from the trap like a pointing finger several hundred feet long. It was set at right angles to the beach, and salmon encountering the lead moved gradually into the trap.

A watchman's shack, containing stove, bunk, food, and cooking utensils, was built on the trap. This year's supplies, as usual, included a rifle, shotgun, revolver, and plenty of ammunition. There was also a skiff which permitted the watchman to escape should a storm threaten the trap's destruction.

"Okay, Duncan, you asked for the trap guard's job, and now you got it," Laird told McArdle when the work was completed. "You know your business. Make suspicious craft keep their distance."

"I won't let you down, Capt'n Errol," McArdle promised.

"Good. I've got every confidence in you, Duncan," Laird replied heartily, then turned somber. "We can't have anything let us down. If we don't get fish now, we'll be pulling out this fall dead broke."

Or just plain dead, Jessie thought worriedly.

★

# Chapter 8

Leaving McArdle to guard the Manitou Point trap, Jessie, Ki, Capt'n Errol, and his crew returned to Glacier Bay to endure the hardest part of a canner's life—the period of uncertainty until the run began. The next few days dragged by, with Laird personally checking the various creeks in the vicinity, hoping to see them alive with fish. But all he, Jessie, and Ki ever saw were a few indolent members of the advance guard.

When Laird could stand it no longer, he boarded a small tender with Jessie and Ki and headed for the Deauville Inlet cannery. Deauville and Oceana were rivals, but friendly, and misery loves company. As Laird explained, many a cannery man had dried another's tears, and in turn had his own dried while waiting for the run.

Five miles from the cannery they spotted one of the Deauville tugs dragging a wallowing scow filled with salmon. They drew alongside the tug, and Laird hailed the skipper, an old acquaintance.

"When did the run start, Gus?" he asked.

"A week ago," Gus replied. Then a look of surprise flashed across his face. "Ain't you gettin' no fish?"

"Nary a one!"

"Somethin' peculiar. Glacier Bay is usually packin' several days before the fish hit Deauville, and this's the biggest run in years. Big fish, too. That scow gen'rally holds forty thousand ordinary salmon. This year thirty-five thousand nearly fills 'er. Maybe somebody cleaned out your trap?" Gus hesitated as Laird shook his head, then blurted out, "Boone Vermillion offered us fifty thousand fish yesterday, wanted eight cents for 'em. The boss just laughed and said he wouldn't take 'em at any price."

"What'd Vermillion do with 'em?" Laird demanded.

Gus shrugged. "I dunno. Saw a big flock of gulls off'n Portage Bay," he added significantly.

Laird headed for Portage Bay.

"It don't make sense," he remarked to Jessie and Ki. "Canneries have to pack fish within forty-eight hours after they're caught. One bad batch—even the rumor of a bad batch—and a cannery is blacklisted f'ever. That don't leave much time for a pirate to peddle his fish, particularly when the cannery is a ways from the scene of his snatch. But Vermillion couldn't towed his fish to Glacier Bay in ample time, and much as he may hate us, he'd surely have sold fish to us rather than take a loss."

"On the other hand," Jessie reminded him, "if Boone Vermillion is playing for big stakes, for Oceana itself, he could afford to take such a loss."

A cloud of gulls, ravens, and eagles lifted into the air as the tender sped into Portage Bay. The beach was lined with dead salmon left by the receding tide. Vermillion had dumped at least fifty thousand! But it would be difficult

104

to make a case of fish piracy against him unless one of his men confessed.

Whatever Vermillion was up to, however, unquestionably the run was on in full. So now, some eighteen hours after leaving the cannery, they returned hopeful of activity. There was not a salmon in the fish house.

"Any word from Duncan McArdle?" Laird asked Foxclaw anxiously.

The superintendent shook his head. "Not yet. Say, all of you look tired, cold, wet. Come to my home, why don't you, and have a cup of coffee. Warm you up. Do you good."

Accepting the invitation, Laird started with Foxclaw for the superintendent's cabin, accompanied by Jessie and Ki. "I'm disgusted with myself," Laird grumbled. "Dad would've figured out the trouble long ago. He never missed."

"Maybe not," Jessie allowed. "But he had experience behind him. We don't know how many mistakes he made when he was our age."

"Well, I can't afford to be making any more."

Entering Foxclaw's cabin, they were met by an Indian woman and a girl of about Jessie's age. "You know my wife," Foxclaw said as he closed the door. "And this is Alice, my daughter. Alice has been away visiting our village."

Mrs. Foxclaw was shorter than her husband and much rounder. A taciturn woman, she evidently felt her task was to supervise the domestic scene, and it was clear that she had done a good job at the cabin, for the grounds about it were neat and the interior a model of traditional Tlingit habitation.

Daughter Alice was an Indian, no doubt about that, with an even tan skin, black eyes and hair, and that saucy air

105

of freedom that came from living in close association with the land. She wore western clothes, with a touch of piping here and there to retain the Indian look, but the two things that type her as Tlingit were the handsome dark braids that hung below her shoulders and the big decorated boots that covered her feet. They gave her otherwise slender body a heavy pinned-to-earth look which matched her pragmatic approach.

While discussing the situation over coffee, Laird spread out a chart on the dining table. The chart was of the bay and nearby coastal region, and he had brought it along to refresh their memory of the contour of the shore. Because salmon were creatures of habit, there were certain possibilities they could eliminate. Salmon returned to the stream of their birth to spawn and die. They didn't go visiting around, and as a general rule they didn't get lost but unerringly returned.

The fish on which Oceana depended spawned in the numerous streams that flowed into Glacier Bay. The run first passed the mouth of Half Moon River, which would have been an ideal spawning stream if it weren't for a waterfall that prevented the fish from swimming upstream. So they continued on into the bay, passing Manitou Point—and ended up in Oceana's floating trap. Of course, to perpetuate the supply, the guard at Manitou Point lifted the trap at stated intervals to permit some fish to continue on to their spawning grounds. The trap, according to Laird, had never been a problem before.

"And I'm not convinced it's the problem now," he said, rolling up the chart. "I think what I ought to do is tour the bay. I'll take a boatload of men around and check out the spawning streams for fish."

"It might not hurt to visit Manitou Point again, thought," Jessie suggested. "After all, if you find fish in any number, the question arises how they could've passed the point without the trap filling."

Laird frowned, Jessie's observation seeming to fill him with unease—as if in spite of his determination to retain faith in Duncan McArdle, he had to confess that perhaps McArdle had been forced or bought by Boone Vermillion into giving over fish from the trap. "Very well," he finally agreed, "but I don't want to make it look like I suspect Duncan in any way. Foxclaw, take the steam dory out to Manitou Point and see what you can see."

"I'll send Alice," Foxclaw said. "Men like to talk with her."

The girl did not smile, and she did not speak. But Ki couldn't help noticing the curt, half-annoyed glance she cast her father. He found her eyes, although cool, somehow provocative, the curve of her lips alluring, just her presence oddly disturbing to his senses.

He blurted, "Y'mean, go alone?"

"Yes." Her voice was low and melodious, in contrast to the sharp appraisal she gave Ki. "Why do you ask?"

"I, ah, I'm interested in your safety," he replied hastily. Jessie rolled her eyes.

Ki wasn't sure if Alice diagnosed Jessie's reaction, but it seemed to him that she smiled. There was just a slight break in her expression, a brief relaxation of the red line of her lips. "I can take care of myself, thank you."

Again Laird frowned. "Well, I'd feel better if you took someone along, Alice. What with Boone Vermillion and his wolves out and about, it could be dangerous in more ways than one to a woman."

Alice eyed Laird scornfully. "I believe I mentioned I can take care of myself."

"You did," her father responded, "but Captain Errol is right. If you go, a man should go with you."

And they all looked expectantly at Ki—all, that is, except Alice. She flushed with indignation, the pupils of her dark eyes dilating.

Wonderful, Ki thought; he'd snookered himself into accompanying a headstrong girl who didn't appear to like him much to begin with, and now resented his intrusion to boot. It promised to be a fun trip.

The fun began early, when they tried to fire up the steam engine on the dory. Klinker-built, the dory was akin to a rowboat in size and stank to high heaven from fish and other dead flesh rotting in its bilge. Amidships squatted the venerable one-lung engine and boiler, rusty and patched, with an encrusted brass plate just over its firebox which read: WICKS, FARMINGHAM, ENGLAND.

The first few attempts to ignite a fire resulted in great eruptions of soot and ash blasting out of the firebox and coating everyone within range a dusty black. Eventually a fire was started, and the asthmatic Wicks was coaxed up to pressure. The lines were cast off, and Alice headed the dory out into the bay while Ki stoked the firebox with wood, watching how she piloted the craft in case he had to take over—and otherwise keeping his distance, in case the girl or the engine decided to explode.

The fun continued; it began to rain, a chilly drizzle.

Luckily they had been sent on their way fully supplied. Now, under their slickers, Alice and Ki were wearing heavy flannel shirts of garish plaid and brown, double-thick canvas pants, waterproofed until they were almost stiff enough to stand alone. They'd also been given blankets, a light belt ax, a glass bottle full of matches, a cooking outfit and a quantity of grub, and a pack board in which to stow the utensils and blankets. Included as well were a couple of Winchester .44-40 repeaters, along with extra ammunition.

As they approached Manitou Point, the rain ceased, the clouds parted, and a burgundy sunset washed Glacier Bay with color. It faded slowly, leaving a final flame on the high crests of the surrounding mountains. Swinging the dory toward the fish trap, they tied up to the platform on which the guard's shack was perched, calling out for Duncan McArdle.

McArdle did not answer.

By now the sunset's last streamers had vanished, replaced by dusk's purple shadows, and there was only a mauve emptiness to be seen around them. Yet it was clear, as they stepped from the dory onto the platform, that there was something wrong, something very wrong. The shanty door hung open on its hinges, and from within came a smell of scorched flesh, bacon grease, powdersmoke, and fish. And it was silent as a tomb.

Ki went first, standing framed on the threshold and raking the dark interior with widening eyes. Alice pressed alongside, and as her pupils adjusted to the gloom, she gasped in horror.

*"Duncan!"*

★

# Chapter 9

Duncan McArdle, stripped nude, sat writhing in ropes that bound him to a chair in front of the potbellied stove. His body was welted with ugly blisters. One glance at the poker jutting from the open stove door told of the torment to which the man had been subjected earlier, when a fire had been burning in the stove and the poker had been sizzling hot.

Hurriedly Ki lit the shack's kerosene lantern. Propping her rifle by the door, Alice strode across and laid a hand sympathetically on the victim's shoulder. McArdle shuddered in violent recoil, moans whining from his flaccid mouth. Ki whipped out his knife and severed the ropes that bound McArdle to the chair and, with Alice, caught him before he could pitch to the floor. Gently they lifted their burden and carried him across the room to the bunk.

"He needs a doctor, Ki."

"Too late."

Alice nodded sadly, realizing Ki was right: Death was

mere moments away. It was then that McArdle opened his eyes for the first time. They were the staring, blank orbs of a person driven insane by unendurable agonies, and they regarded Alice with a wild intensity that was pitiful to see. Glancing about the shack for something— anything—that might help, Alice found a flask of whiskey on a shelf and brought it to the bunk, giving McArdle a long swig of the raw, fiery liquor. Emitting a slavering moan then, he managed to bring his eyes into focus—a focus that reflected impending death. Feebly he croaked for another snort and then tried to speak.

"They came . . . Didn't hear them . . ."

"Who, Duncan? Who came?"

"D-don't know how they got so close. . . ." McArdle's eyes revolved in their sockets, the cheap whiskey having taken hold of him and rousing his flagging vitality. "I didn't hear a thing. They m-must've drifted down with the tide."

"Who? Were they Vermillion's men, Duncan?"

"They shoot. I shoot, three times, then they . . ." A paroxysm racked McArdle's naked form. "I'm tired . . . can't think. I sleep, then . . . I—" His convulsing muscles suddenly went limp.

Alice leaned over him, thumbing an eyelid, then bent an ear to his still chest. Straightening, she said, "He's gone to sleep."

"Yes," Ki said quietly. "The big sleep."

Bleakly Alice began wrapping McArdle in the bunk's blanket. "We must take him back to the cannery now, see that he's buried proper."

Ki shook his head. "I'm not so sure."

"What?" Alice looked appalled. "You'd deny the poor soul—"

"Easy, easy. Of course we're taking McArdle back, but

112

maybe not just yet," Ki explained. "Look, think about what happened here. McArdle wasn't killed defending the trap against gents pirating fish—there aren't any fish in the trap to fight over, much less die over. No, he was tortured to death and left here to be found as an example."

"Even if that were so, Ki, I still don't see—"

"*Think*, Alice!" Ki cut in again. "One example won't make much difference. But if the next couple of guards befall a similar fate, nobody'll be willing to stay here on duty. No more trap would spell the end of Oceana. For us right now, though, it means whoever did this to McArdle may be lying in ambush for us, just waiting to catch us on our way back to the cannery."

"Well, it sure means we can't stay here, either!"

"And that leads to my second point. I think we should head the other way, go out and find the salmon that seem to've vanished before reaching here. I think we should begin at Half Moon River, and if they're coming in there, then we return to the cannery. If not, keep going."

"They can't be running at Half Moon River! That's impossible!"

"There's an old saying—British, I believe—that goes: Once all the probabilities are eliminated, then whatever is left, no matter how impossible, must be the answer," Ki replied. "Besides—"

"Shh!" Alice cupped her ear, listening intently. "Douse the light, quick!" Then, as Ki hastened to blow out the kerosene lamp, she grabbed her Winchester and ducked outside, closing the door noiselessly behind her.

Crossing to the window and peering out, Ki tried to follow the girl's lithe silhouette as she headed out along the trapline. But she disappeared almost at once, her dark shadow melding silently with the gloom of the moonless night. Then he heard what Alice must have heard—oars rattling and a boat bumping against the platform piling.

Suddenly a blinding light flooded the shack. "Don't move," a gravelly voice bellowed through a megaphone. "We've got you covered!"

For a moment Ki stood rigid. A second voice said, "Wal, wal, the cannery ran outta men. They're using Chinks."

Ki made a sudden dive for his rifle and rolled into the corner of the shack. Buckshot splintered through the thin boards of the shack walls, and some of it tore through Ki's slicker. Levering the Winchester, he poked it through a hole in the shack and tried to see his attackers. The blinding light full in his eyes shut out everything but the bow of the boat nosing the platform. He raised his rifle slightly and triggered; the light vanished and he heard the clatter of glass.

Something droned through the shack. A rifle roared. Several more opened up, and each time a metal-jacketed bullet drilled through both walls and splashed into the water beyond the trap. Ki returned fire as fast as he could, forcing the attackers to keep to their boat, below the level of the platform. An oil-soaked torch blossomed in the night as one of them hurled a firebrand to the roof.

Instantly a shot rang out as Ki, shifting locations, fired his rifle. The torch-wielding gunman, arms windmilling, plunged into the water. A sharp salvo of gunfire now burst in the night as the raiders opened fire to avenge the death of one of their number. By the glare of the blazing torch that was igniting the roof, Ki aimed returning blasts at silhouetted men.

Another raider spun and fell. Discerning details was very difficult in the morass of swirling shadow and flickering light outside, and vision was worsening as choking, eye-stinging smoke began curling down from the smoldering roof shingles. But Ki knew he hadn't shot, and then it seemed to him that in rapid succession came two more reports from some weapon in back and to one side of the raiders' boat. The sharp cracks coincided with two more gunmen crumpling violently, blood spluttering from their mortal wounds as they fell into the water. Startled curses rippled along the bunched line of raiders. But now, inside the shack, Ki realized what must be happening. Alice was darting about the trapline with her Winchester repeater, boldly sniping at close range, trusting that the confused bedlam of conflict would protect her from discovery.

"Hot damn!" Grabbing a large, empty stewpot off the stove, Ki bolted for the door. Outside on the platform he hurled a ladder against the eaves, scooped up a potful of water, and climbed the ladder. A wedge of raiders began scrambling from the boat to the platform, eager to cut him down, an open target at easy range.

And out of nowhere stabbed the blasts of Alice's rifle. Her concentrated defense routed the chargers, smashing one from the platform and wounding two others before the raiders could retreat to the concealment of their boat. As they tried to reorganize for a second attack, Ki doused the blaze, scrambled down the ladder, and sprinted safely back inside the shack. After barricading the door, he took a moment to reload his Winchester. Then he joined Alice in renewing gunfire.

Outside, the raiders were increasingly faltering in disarray. They had not expected such fierce resistance. Nor had they expected to be caught in a crossfire, snagged between the cabin and someone stalking behind them and picking them off with unerrring lead.

The Winchester materialized again with a fiery discharge, only to vanish phantomlike as another raider keeled into the bay. Inside the shack, Ki let loose a barrage whenever he saw the fleeting shadow of a raider along the rim of the platform. The once-smug gang fought stubbornly, then desperately, finally crumbling into pandemonium, until Ki heard the voice of one gunnie shout loudly, "Shove off, men! We're losing too many!"

The raiders, clambering in the boat, began rowing frantically away from the trap. Ki could make out the raiding craft now, a darker shadow against the shadows of night. They raced for open water, their flanks harried by raking shots until they were out of gun range . . . and then a strange hush descended around the shack, broken only by the rhythmic splash of water against the pilings. Ki edged out onto the platform, crouching with rifle in hand.

Nothing disturbed the quiet.

"They're gone, Alice. It may be a trick."

Alice, balancing gracefully, padded in along the bobbing trapline. There was a feral glint to her eyes, and perspiration beaded her forehead. Ki didn't know whether it was the cold sweat of fear or the heat of excitement.

"Those beasts," she whispered savagely. "Those dirty beasts! Well, we taught them an expensive lesson and perhaps evened the score a little for poor Duncan McArdle."

"They'll be back," Ki reckoned. "In cattle country rustlers take a battle in stride and come back again as soon as they reorganize their forces. I figure fish pirates are as tough a breed."

Alice nodded. "But we won't be here. We won't be going to the cannery, either, crossing the bay where they can attack us." She stared implacably at Ki with adamantine eyes. "We're heading for Half Moon River, just like you suggested. Let's get Duncan's body aboard and cast off right away!"

Their trip to Half Moon River took the rest of the night. Rather than going the simplest, most direct route across open water, Alice ran the dory close along the shoreline, following the meandering contour of the land. They held to the shadows, traveling slowly, trying to keep the boat's wake and the flatulent *phut-phutt* of the old engine as low as possible, stopping only in sheltered coves when replenishing firewood or fresh water for the boiler.

They spoke little, and only in subdued tones. Sometimes, though, as they sat together, the sway of the boat would cause Alice to bump against Ki. After the first few times Ki grew aware that her knee would nudge his thigh, and that she would lean near, faintly smiling in a tantalizing manner. And he began to get the idea that she was getting ideas.

Pale streaks of light were slashing through the brightened eastern sky when they neared the mouth of Half Moon River. Now more than ever they kept a sharp lookout, aware that at any moment a rifle might be drawing a bead on them, their only warning a shot crashing out on the still air. But as they rounded a low headland, an alarming scene of a wilder sort greeted their eyes.

Hundreds of leaping salmon were in the air, proof that hundreds of thousands swam below the surface. It was incredible that after countless generations of salmon had passed Manitou Point and fought their way down Glacier Bay to spawn, they would attempt to go up Half Moon River. And yet, if Ki and Alice could believe their eyes, the fish had suddenly decided to change age-old habits.

"I've never seen such a concentration of salmon off the mouth of a river," Alice observed, awestruck. As she piloted toward the beach, she and Ki could feel the dory slice through silvery bodies, and when they looked back, the foam of their wake was flecked with crimson. There were hundreds of dead and dying fish on the beach, and flocks of sea gulls and land birds were gorging themselves.

117

After dropping anchor, they waded ashore. The river was alive with salmon, the grass along both banks crimson with blood where bears had been fishing. Proceeding with caution, having no desire to encounter a she-bear with cubs, they headed upstream toward the waterfall.

The river flowed out through a gorge, steeply sloped, hopper-shaped, overgrown with conifers and brushy thickets. The gorge grew narrower, becoming almost a tunnel by the time they reached the base of the falls. There, a pool worn into the rock was supplied by a surging torrent splashing hundreds of feet from a boulder- and log-jammed lip. And there, as well, salmon were leaping from the choked pool, striking the water and falling back. They kept at it until exhausted, then the current rolled them over belly-up and carried them off. But there were others to take their place.

"It's crazy," Alice murmured.

Thoughtfully, Ki glanced up at the rim of the falls. "Might be worth having a look above, just for luck. You feel up to it?"

"I won't fall down, don't worry." Alice smiled but went on speaking, as if she had not paused again to brush against him. "But then, I imagine you aren't much for worrying. You take things as they come, as they are."

Ki could have kissed her, sensing Alice wanted to learn what his mouth might feel like on her lips. But he didn't, wary of what her game was, why she had seemingly changed her attitude toward him. Instead he merely grinned and started up the grade that would lead to the bluff overlooking the falls—and glimpsed the frown that came and went so suddenly on her face. Apparently the superintendent's daughter was not one to be trifled with, especially when she hankered to do some trifling of her own.

118

It was a stiff, dangerous climb over slippery rocks and through brushy scrub, the ascent made all the more difficult by their cumbersome rifles, which they carried slung across their backs. And increasingly could be heard an uneasy moaning in the tops of great firs and cedars as a freshening wind came down from the summits. The trail they forged pitched sharply upward, with many turns and switchbacks forced by the rugged lay of the land, and they feared they would not be over the worst of their climb before the threatening storm broke. Indeed, presently the sun was blotted by overcast and grayish shadows melted into a gloom which crept through the deep woods, growing thicker every minute. Soon there came a whispering murmur from ahead, and they knew that it was rain, for they could make out blue-black clouds sweeping down from the heights.

The storm had not yet broken, however, when they finally gained the crest and could move toward the falls. They entered a tangle of shrubs and trees, whose windswept limbs were twisted in every conceivable angle. The cluttered forest of conifers and hardwoods was densest at the water's edge, where Alice and Ki paused, staring perplexed at the salmon swimming about.

"Crazier and crazier," Alice said, shaking her head in bewilderment. "Nobody carried them up here, but here they are."

Carefully they forded the stream and worked their way down the opposite bank. Several salmon shot through the swift, clear water. It seemed to Ki that they emerged from brush overhanging the bank. He crawled over the brush and peered down.

Several short flumes connected wooden tanks supported on rods driven into the solid rock. The tanks and flumes were cleverly concealed by the brush, so Ki couldn't see for sure if they extended all the way down from the falls' rim to the pool below; he was positive they did, though, for salmon were rushing up the flumes, resting briefly in the tanks, then continuing on to the top. It was an improvised fish ladder permitting fish to get around the falls, but as Alice observed when she took a look, it was one of the most effective she had ever seen. There was only one flaw. This was the year of a big run, and the volume was so great the ladder couldn't handle it all. That explained the congestion below.

"Unless I'm a heap mistook, this's the doing of Boone Vermillion," Ki said as they eased from the brushy overhang. "He's killing two birds with one stone here, not only preventing fish from reaching the Manitou Point trap, which spells ruin for Laird, but also creating a new spawning grounds."

Stepping back from the bank, then, they were skirting a stand of trees when from the murky woods a voice said, "Well, now, jus' where d'you reckon you're going?"

They stopped, careful to make no play for their rifles. Out from the trees, astride a bay, rode a swarthy man in dirt-crusted garb, curly black hair peeking out from the open neck of his shirt and from beneath his sweat-stained hat. He had spoken pleasantly enough, but his eyes were as hard as bottler glass, and his right thumb was hooked in his sagging gunbelt, an inch or so above the butt of a .45.

"Merely passing through," Ki answered, affably nervous, fiddling open the clasps of his slicker. "We must've gotten lost a dozen times so far. Hard on my wife, her in the family way and all."

It was then, abruptly, that the storm struck. Seemingly out of nowhere it hit with a sudden steady rain, no thunder or lightning or threshing of wind, just a heavy sodden downpour.

"Je-sus!" The man scowled annoyed. "Let's get it done before we're drown-ded!"

Two more men suddenly dived from the surrounding bush. They'd been sneaking around in a flanking attack, that much was obvious to Ki—just as obvious as the motives of the swarthy man who, seeing his opportunity, drew his revolver while charging directly at Alice. Alice fumbled to unsling her rifle, but she had no chance to defend herself in time.

Nor, apparently, had Ki. The other two men landed in front of and beside him, swiveling to fire. The one in front shot. But Ki had already reacted; ignoring his rifle, he'd dipped in his open slicker to his vest and flicked a *shuriken* star-blade a split second sooner. The woods resounded with the revolver's report, the man's bullet spanging off a boulder. Then he sank rolling on the ground, choking and gasping, a star-shaped disk protruding from his throat.

The second man stared disbelievingly, then blinked as flashes of metal whizzed through the air before his eyes. A *shuriken* slashed high into his abdomen, and another, better placed, sliced like a scalpel between his ribs and imbedded itself in the man's heart. He collapsed atop his throat-slit pal.

"Fuck!" the swarthy man snarled, struggling to get in an accurate shot with his pistol while shielding himself with Alice's twisting body. "Hold it!" he warned, dragging her closer to him. "You try'n snicker-snee me, buddy, an' the bitch earns it!"

Helpless, Ki watched the swarthy man jab the muzzle of his pistol into the nape of her neck. Alice was still writhing frantically, her mouth widening to scream. The man rashly clamped a hand over her face, and she bit his palm. Now it was the man who screamed, letting go.

Immediately Alice plunged headlong to the ground,

121

scrambling for her fallen rifle. The man fired. Ki felt the bullet rip along his right arm, shredding the sleeve of his slicker as he let loose another *shuriken*. There was an explosive grunt as the man topped backward from his saddle, the *shuriken* buried in his upper left pectorals. Using his horse for cover, he sprinted through the rain into a thin but rugged strip of boulders that bordered the falls.

"Stay flat!" Ki ordered Alice, launching after the man. He saw a gunbarrel poke around the peak of a boulder, and with an abrupt surge to the left, he dived behind a fallen pine tree just as a gunshot gouged splinters overhead. The shot placed the man for him. He began inching noiselessly through the rocks and brush toward that position.

"You shit!" the man yelled. "You goddamned shit!" He fired again, furrowing a second white gash of bare wood through the darker bark of the pine.

Ki paused, gauging by the voice and shot that the man was retreating softly toward the edge of the falls. There were only a few yards separating him and the man, but they consisted of a thick fence of briers, boulders, and trees. No open space for pitching *shuriken* blades or his throwing daggers. He continued to ease nearer, quietly unsheathing his short, curve-bladed *tanto*. It was his best choice now, deadly in hand-to-hand combat.

"I'll kill you! You'n the cunt, y'hear?"

Ki leaped toward the voice, a steely grin etched on his face as he bounded from boulder to boulder across the uneven ground. He could hear a shuffling in the underbrush ahead as the man swiveled to bring his revolver to bear. He pivoted off the slope of a rock, sighting the man by the rim. The man was bleeding, wheezing, but he had a lethal glint to his eyes, a firmness to his stance, as he trained his revolver. Ki scarcely had an instant's grace to dart aside before the revolver lanced flame and lead ricocheted off the rocks next to him in a shower of sparks.

Instantly Ki lunged forward, slashing underhanded with his knife. The blade bit into the man's belly, and Ki sliced upward through his brisket as though gutting an animal. Warm blood gushed over the hilt and his hand.

The man teetered away, off the blade, and spun over the edge in a long fall to the pool below. Ki peered down from the rimrock at the splayed body, facedown in the river, rocking gently from the current and fish roiling around it. Then he turned and wearily started back.

Alice stood hunched in the rain, head lowered, both hands on her knees.

"It's over," Ki said gently, patting her shoulder. "Now, let's get out of this storm."

The rain, growing windblown with terrific velocity, was coming in torrents, drenching them as they hurried for the shelter of a wide-spreading cedar. So ferocious was the downfall that Ki knew a cloudburst must have occurred among the higher peaks.

Huddling there, waiting for the storm to pass, Alice shook her head in disgust at her own behavior. Her color grew better, and she decided she wasn't going to be sick. "I'm sorry. It's silly of me, but it got on my nerves. These men, and the men at Manitou Point, they wanted to kill us."

"Vermillion wanted to kill us. They were just obeying orders."

She snuggled closer. "And I said I could take care of myself," she whispered contritely. A shiver rippled through her. Ki conjured up things to say that might comfort her, but she kissed him before he could open his mouth.

It was an affectionate kiss at first, lazy and teasing.

Then it changed, and a smoldering passion seemed to take fire in her. She pressed against him, squirming and rubbing, her mouth like a bitter fruit that would give a man pain when he tasted it.

Ki knew she was scared and dejected and in need of the support he could give her. But he wasn't sure she needed to be given the support that was hardening in response to her torrid kiss—not here, anyway, not yet. So after a moment of tight-locking lips, he drew back and said reluctantly, "Whoa up."

She tilted her head. "Is it Miss Starbuck? Is it some other woman?"

"Not Jessie, no, and not any woman."

"Well, if no woman's got you by the totem pole, Ki, why're you balking at my offer?" She nuzzled his chest, her eyes mocking. "I owe you. I've only one thing of value, so I'm paying. With interest."

"Great. I'll collect later."

"The debt is due now." With open mouth and slowly sliding tongue, she kissed him again, lazily, sensuously. "I'm not a white society belle, all coyness and honey," she murmered. "I'm a widow, my husband killed in a hunting accident. Short-lived, short-loved, and I decided when I returned to my village to go after what I felt like having when I feel like having it. And I willingly admit it."

"Bluntly, too."

"If there's anything frontier native life does, it strips away the nonessentials." And with that Alice stripped off her clothes. Humming provocatively, she removed her slicker and pulled her flannel shirt over her head. Her canvas pants went next, down to her knees. Her firm, plump breasts swayed gracefully as she sat down on her slicker and drew off each pantleg and boot. Naked save for her drawers, she grabbed for Ki's pants. "What's keeping you?"

Ki felt that tug all the way through his taut loins. He needed Alice like he needed a bad case of poison ivy, but he supposed that was what made men different from women. When a woman was wanting, a man will somehow rise to the occasion. Besides, they weren't going anywhere till the gale blew over.

He reached for her and got a handful of thin white cotton. Drawers off and gone, Alice crushed her body to his, kissing with hot, moist urgency. She helped him out of his clothes, then pushed him slowly down, kissing his neck and ears, until he was lying on his back. Then, working lower, hot and moist, she laved his chest and stomach, teased his navel, and dipped to the insides of his thighs. She kissed him wetly there, let her tongue drag on his skin, and then, when the tension was unbearable, she went down on him open-mouthed, wide, hot, trying to swallow all of his girth. She slid her hands under his hips and encouraged his movements, giving with his upward thrusts, taking as much as she could. The roof of her mouth was ridged and hard, and her soft palate behind the hardness was a tantalyzing thrill. Her tongue was rough, teasing his sensitivity. Then she swallowed the length of him, down until her nose was against his groin, and back his entire length to repeat, and repeat again.

Ki could feel a tumultous eruption building, building in his scrotum. Too soon, he thought, too soon . . . Forcing himself to break free, he twisted up and around, planting his knees between her squirming thighs, feeling her ready and wet with yearning anticipation.

Reaching between them, Alice grasped his turgid shaft with one hand, using her other hand to fondle her pubes and spread them for his entry. Ki sank forward, entering her with her guidance, feeling her grip around his entire length with a firmness that almost drove him crazy. Alice sang out her delight, her arms wrapping tightly around his back, pulling him down against her breasts, her body following his rhythm in wild abandonment. Her nails began digging spasmodically, slithering down to claw at the flesh of his pumping buttocks, thrusting him deeper into her while her thighs splayed wide on the slicker beneath her.

Satisfying Alice's ravenous needs was exhausting. Snaking his tongue inside her mouth, Ki hoped to calm her briefly and regain his strength. It was a futile attempt. More frenziedly now, she locked her ankles firmly around him, her nude flesh slippery from the sweat of her burgeoning passion. Arching her buttocks, she humped up and down, undulating slowly at first, then faster, faster—until finally every sensation surging within their bodies was expelled, and they collapsed, satiated. . . .

She chuckled contentedly. "How's that for my payback?"

"In full," Ki said, mustering the energy to ease out of her.

After some while they sensed a tentative ebbing to the storm. They made love again and then, as the wind began to die noticeably, and the downpour gradually tapered to a shower, they went out naked and washed in the rain before dressing. Increasingly the sky lightened, the shower lessened. When they could glimpse the dim, sulphurous glow of the sun again, they decided the worst of the storm was over and it was time to go.

They headed back down to the beach, leaving the fish ladder undisturbed, figuring it might well prove valuable to Oceana at some future time. But the most important question remained unanswered: What was diverting the salmon from Manitou Point and the bay to Half Moon River?

They boarded the dory and drove it slowly through the massed salmon, then stopped and studied the scene. Water from a nearby glacial stream clouded the area and obscured everything a foot or two below the surface. But it seemed to them that the area of leaping fish ended very abruptly. Too abruptly, as if something turned them back "as a fence turns back cattle," Ki remarked. They cruised along the outer area. Except for casual fish leaping, it was well defined.

"A line of piles driven out from the shore," Alice reflected, "and strung with netting would turn the fish into Half Moon River."

"I think you've hit on it," Ki agreed. "And if the tops were cut off below the surface, nobody would ever guess piling existed. Let's check it out, Alice. Drive into the fish area, lower the anchor, and drive back out."

Following Ki's suggestion, Alice looped through the mass of salmon with the anchor down about fifteen feet. As they headed outward, the anchor fouled in something. Ki got the anchor line around a windlass and hauled it up tight, but after that he couldn't budge it.

The tide was rising, so they sat back and waited to see whether the anchor would give way or the stern of the boat would go under. The stern settled nearly a half hour before the anchor broke clear. Ki hauled it up and found strands of webbing fouled on the flukes.

"Start stoking and keep our steam up," Alice ordered, heading for Glacier Bay. "There's no time to lose." She full-throttled the old one-lunger Wicks, wrenched briefly at the reversing lever, and winced at the resulting clatter of worn gears. "We have to get that hidden trap cleared away and all those fish released. Salmon don't wait, and Capt'n Laird can't delay!"

★

# Chapter 10

Everyone was on hand when Ki and Alice arrived back at the cannery. Ki gave a brisk account of the events, beginning with the death of McArdle, passing over the lovemaking with Alice, and ending with a description of the fish ladder and the hidden netting. Alice said little, remaining poker-faced throughout the edited version of their time together. In turn they learned, to no surprise, that the trip Jessie, Laird, and crew had taken around the bay had proved futile. Their own news created not only alarm but relief as well, for the apparent lack of salmon had stirred up a hectic time at the cannery.

"I'm glad you're alive," Laird told them. "Everything else has gone to hell, and I've been fearing the worst. Now I've an idea." Leading the way to the machine shop, he sketched a design for the blacksmith and scribbled dimensions. "Make me some hooks like that as soon as you can," he directed.

The cannery crew watched all this with suspicious scrutiny. According to Foxclaw, they doubted Laird's ability to handle the situation, and there was unrest among them. "They want to go back to Seattle, Capt'n Errol," the superintendent reported gloomily. "Boone Vermillion has got troublemakers planted among them, if you ask me. They're convincing the crew that you're going broke and they won't get their pay."

"Tell 'em we'll have fish inside forty-eight hours," Laird said briskly. Then, while the blacksmith was making the hooks and others were gathering the gear they would need, he called together the old-time hands who had fought many a battle with his father. Briefly he explained what lay ahead. "I'm not asking any man to serve under me for this," he concluded. "Someone may get hurt or even killed. You don't need to be afraid of your jobs if you don't go along. They're secure. Is that plain?"

"Plain and damned fair," Hawser Yokum declared. "I'm into it to the ears."

Everyone wanted to be included, and Laird selected a dozen of the best—men he had reason to believe would prove quick thinkers and who could handle themselves in a rough-and-tumble fight.

"Maybe there won't be no fight," Pierre Quinotte said gloomily.

"There'll be one, okay," Laird assured him. "I'm not a gambling man, but I'd bet five to one that by now Vermillion knows his three guards at Half Moon River are dead. Meaning he knows we're on to his trickery there, and the time for a showdown has come. Now, you boys pile onto the tug," he ordered, then turned to the superintendent. "Foxclaw, send a couple of tenders and scows over to Half Moon River. You take the launch and head out for Bismark Cove. There're some purse seiners starving to death because the traps are choked with fish.

Charter 'em for a week and send 'em to Half Moon River. We're going to have fish."

Standing by listening, Jessie calculated that if all went well, the tug would arrive first, followed by the purse seiners. The scows would come limping along last. What she had not figured on was Laird objecting to her presence.

"You stay here at the cannery, where it's safe," he told Jessie. "Where we're going is no place for a lady."

"A lady is a lady wherever she is," Jessie retorted icily, as though that somehow answered his protests, and she stalked up the gangplank, onto the tug.

Glancing at Ki, who gave a sympathetic shrug, Laird sighed the sigh of men plagued by women. . . .

Arriving at Half Moon River, Laird was so astonished at the sight of all the trapped fish thrashing about that at first he wanted to steam right on across the underwater netting. But on second thought he realized there was too much chance of hitting a pile and knocking a hole in the hull. Instead, he dropped anchor just outside the netting and lowered two dinghies.

As the dinghies, carrying men and hooks, moved away from the tug, those aboard paid out heavy lines attached to the hooks. The process was simple: The hooks were dropped beyond the fence, then the tug pulled them through the webbing and ripped open wide holes. This process would be repeated until the channel was clear.

The men had almost finished placing the anchors when two fast launches loaded with men steamed out from shore.

"Here they come!" Laird yelled. "Let the anchors go and come back to the tug!"

As soon as the anchors settled, the tug moved ahead, taking up the slack. Jessie saw Jack Wing and Fantan

131

Monger in one craft and Boone Vermillion in the other. "I guess Vermillion hasn't forgotten that pasting you gave him in Seattle," she said to Laird. "Looks like he wants to settle the score personally."

"My pleasure," Laird replied with grim relish. Then, as the first of his dinghies came alongside the tug, he called to Ki, "Stay here, help fend off any of these bastards who try boarding the tug!" And he leapt into the dinghy, shouting to its crew, "They're going to cut the anchor lines! Pile into 'em!"

A moment later four boats met with a resounding clatter, and the fight was on.

As Jack Wing slashed at the nearest line with his knife, Laird smashed his fist against the man's jaw and sent him headlong into the water. A couple of Vermillion's men grasped him before he sank, and struggled mightily to boost him back aboard, coughing and cursing. Someone broke an oar over Laird's head, and he went down heavily but shook off the fog, picked up the handle portion of the oar, and waded in again.

Fantan Monger, with another broken oar, was knocking Oceana men right and left. Laird watched his chance and smashed the oar-wielder across the Adam's apple. Monger howled like a wolf, hurled his oar into the air, howled again, and pulled a revolver from a shoulder holster.

"That gun's full of water!" Laird yelled. "Watch out, boys, it may explode!"

As Monger, tricked by Laird's shout, shook his pistol, Laird hurled an oar as a man would throw a spear. The end struck Monger's chest, and he catapulted over the side, rocking the launch so violently that it sent the floundering Jack Wing back into the water, along with both men who were trying to help him. Laird, bracing himself, turned to continue the fight—and a Vermillion man clobbered him

132

with a hardwood peavey, and Laird dropped again, dazed senseless.

Meanwhile, Vermillion's second launch was ramming against the tug, his men trying to swarm aboard. Pandemonium reigned, with shouts, screams of the wounded, the swift blastings of guns. Wisely, Vermillion himself stayed toward the stern of the launch, urging his men up and onward while keeping an eye on how things were going on his other launch. Seeing Laird knocked senseless to its deck seemed to galvanize him, as though here was the chance he had been lusting for. He leapt to the other craft's slanting deck, revolver in hand, his mouth a wicked slit as he bore down on his hapless victim.

Ki, too, saw what had occurred, but he could do nothing to help. A Vermillion man had him point-blank in the sights of a pistol, the man's chinless face leering with the desire to kill.

It was the last smile he made. Before the chinless man could squeeze the trigger, Ki went into action. Abruptly stabbing the man's throat between the forefinger and middle finger of his left hand, Ki crushed the man's windpipe, crumpling him instantly to the ground. Simultaneously he sent a *shuriken* speeding toward another Vermillion man, a short tubby man who was trying to catch hold of Jessie.

In the split second it took for Ki to attack, Jessie flattened herself to the deck, glimpsing the *shuriken* slicing into the short man's neck. Rolling, she came up with her pistol clutched in her right hand.

Other Vermillion raiders, seeing their short pal go down, triggered lead in a haphazard if concerted roar, trying desperately to butcher Ki. But Ki was not there. Springing high across the deck, he lashed out with a leaping kick, catching one man in the solar plexus. Clutching his hemorrhaging

133

belly, the man fell to his knees, mimicking the short man, who'd crumpled hunched over as though he were praying, the *shuriken* protruding from his blood-spurting larynx.

Jessie blew a hole through the chest of another man before he could target Ki again in his gunsights, and as yet another man swiveled for a shot, she fired again. A sudden lurch of the tug, however, spoiled her aim, and the bullet merely creased the man's shoulder without stopping him. It did distract him, though, giving Ki the time he needed. He dived across the short distance, using a *mae geri keage*—a forward snap-kick—followed by a *yoko hija ate*—a sideways elbow smash—to cave in the man's ribs and stop his heart.

The Vermillion men were burly hardcases, picked for brawling and mauling, but, nevertheless, the fight appeared to be going against the fish pirate. His men, sensing this, counting their casualties, began retreating back onto their launch. The battle was not yet over, but it seemed to Ki that for the moment Jessie was fairly safe—at least, safer than Errol Laird was—and Jessie agreed.

"Don't worry about me, Ki! Get Errol!"

Jumping from the tug down to the launch, Ki elbowed, punched, and kicked his way to its stern. From there he sprang across to the other launch, much as Vermillion had done a moment earlier, landing just in time to hear Vermillion rage at Laird:

"This's been long in coming, you sonofabitch!"

Ki tensed, seeing Laird struggling woozily to his knees. He felt the impact of a wave against the launch; a sheet of spray filled the air and struck Vermillion squarely, upsetting his aim, and the shot went wild. Ki hurled himself across the launch, landing on Vermillion. Breath was expelled in painful gasps from Vermillion as he flattened face-first to the deck, but he was still game, wrenching around with an oath and swinging up his gunhand.

Laird caught his wrist and drove it to the deck, twisting the weapon from his hand. Palming its butt, finger on the trigger, Laird stuck the muzzle of the gun into Vermillion's ear. "You bet it's been long in coming," he snarled. "Move, damn you! Make a twitch! I'm cravin' you to!"

Vermillion turned to stone—to a craven-eyed statue of blanch-white marble.

Seeing their boss captured had a marked effect on his men. Already shaken by the ferocity of the Oceana crew, those few left on the launch joined Jack Wing and Fantan Monger and others in the water, where half swimming, half thrashing, they fled for the second launch, which was pulling away from the tug. Deserted, the injured sullenly surrendered.

Now in command of one of Vermillion's launches, Laird piloted the craft alongside the tug. He grinned up at Jessie, then ordered his crew: "Take care of the wounded, tie 'em hand and foot, then collect the dead and dump 'em all aboard the launch. I'll detail a crew to ship the whole mess of 'em back to the cannery, while the rest of us—"

Suddenly he and Ki saw horror in Jessie's eyes, and whirled. Boone Vermillion was leveling a derringer, his face congealed with hate and desperation. Laird struggled to swing his revolver around, knowing he was too late. An instant quicker Ki took a step and, as the hideaway gun spat flame, kicked Vermillion in the chin, almost breaking the man's neck and cracking his skull as his head hit the deck.

Jessie winced and crumpled against the rail.

"She's hit!" someone yelled, and pivoting, Ki scrambled up to the tug and caught her dead weight in his arm.

135

"It's nothing," she gasped, managing a smile. "My arm. Just got grazed, is all."

"Is all!" Laird roared from the launch and locked with Vermillion. They rolled, Vermillion coming up on top, breaking loose and trying to dive overboard. Laird tripped him, and when Vermillion tried to get up, he knocked him back down. And repeated it again and again, until Vermillion was a moaning, beaten figure at his feet.

"D-don't kill me," Vermillion whimpered. "I got a wife and children—"

"No doubt your wife and children would be better off if you were dead," Laird rasped. He paused, as if sensing he was out of control with bloodlust. Then, glancing at the milling fish behind the net, he turned back to Vermillion, his voice as hard as the shine in his eyes. "All right. You'n me got things to talk over, like how the *Hecate* sunk, and how McArdle was murdered. But it'll have to wait. We got fishin' to do, damn quick, and a damn lot of it, and I ain't about to work with my back turned to you or your dock-whollopers, Vermillion. I'm puttin' you on ice till I can deal with you later, when I got the time and where I got the place to deal good'n properly."

Raising no resistance, Vermillion and his remaining men were bound with ropes and placed under armed guard—three Oceana crewmen picked by Laird, along with some who'd been injured. Because her flesh wound, though minor, nonetheless needed treatment, Jessie finally relented to accompany those in the launch back to the cannery.

Laird let out a sigh of relief as he watched the launch steam off across the bay. "I feel better with her out of harm's way," he told Ki when the craft had passed from view. "Now, let's tend to that netting!"

136

# Chapter 11

Picking up work where they'd left off, Oceana crewmen again rowed out in dinghies and snagged the hooks in place. The tug, turning on the power, tore a big gash in the hidden fence, then reversed so that the hooks could be reset once more—and so on, the men working slowly toward the shore, tearing away the webbing. Below them, they knew, the salmon were moving toward Manitou Point, where an Oceana hand named Scanlon had taken over McArdle's duties as trap guard.

As they finished, Laird and Ki went to the wheelhouse and scanned the nearby waters. Two purse seiners were steaming toward them. In the distance could be seen a tender and scows, manned by the rest of the *Snohomish* deckhands, old and new, and the more adventurous of the cannery crew. When shortly the seiners passed, Laird yelled, then pointed. Spreading their nets in the center of the salmon off Half Moon River, the two seiners circled, brought the ends of the net together, hauled away until the bottom closed, then waited until a scow was nudged alongside.

Loading the scow was a tedious, grueling operation. When the scow was at last piled mountainously with salmon and wallowed low in the water, the tug moved in to tow it to the cannery while the smaller tender waited to shuttle another empty scow into position. It took almost till sunset before the scow was hooked up, but finally the tug picked up the slack in the short-coupled wire cable and gathered grudging way.

They started out making good time, considering. Close to four knots, the tug settling back on her haunches for the long pull through the bay, and Half Moon River was falling gradually astern when suddenly Pierre Quinotte cried out:

*"Sacrebleu, m'sieurs! Regardez!"*

Eyes followed his pointing finger and fastened on a red glow hanging over the trees. Laird swore.

"Careless hunters or prospectors again! Looks like someone let their campfire spread into the timber. Between 'em and idjit lumberjacks, there won't be a tree left a-standing, I swear!"

Ki hardly heard as he studied that glow. It seemed to him that it was too restricted for a timber fire, and he was instinctively troubled by it lying in the direction they were going—the same course Jessie's launch had taken. But there was nothing except the vague unease he felt, and he was wondering whether to even bring it up when his eye happened to catch something else—something that the flicker of the distant blaze, reflecting off the choppy water, just chanced to highlight for an instant. He started aft for a closer look, then changed his mind and turned to Laird.

"I'm of mind to take a little jaunt in a dinghy, perhaps across to the scow. Care to join me?"

It sounded casual. So casual that Laird cast him a very hard glance, pondering, and called to his wheelman, "Keep her heading the way she is till we get back." Then motioning to Ki, he headed for the boat deck.

When they got there, they saw one of the new hands, a bearded, buck-toothed sailor named Ferguson, already had a dinghy cleared away, and part of the scow gang standing by the falls. Ferguson gestured to a couple of the gang as Laird and Ki came up. "You two," he said. "You look like you could pull an oar."

"They can stay aboard, mister," Laird told Ferguson. "We'll take over for them."

Ferguson's Adam's apple rose and fell. "That won't be necessary, Capt'n Errol," he said. "It's just a routine chore."

"That's me," Laird said pleasantly. "Routine Rollo. They'll stay here."

Ferguson hesitated, his eyes measuring Laird and Ki carefully. Then whatever he had in mind passed, and he shot a look at the two men he had appointed for the rowing detail. Ki wondered what that look meant. Well, there was no better way of finding out. Following Laird, he climbed over the gunwale and settled himself in the stern sheets. The crew lowered the dingy away. He fended off from the tug's side as Laird and Ferguson took up the oars.

With the strain eased on the cable, the scow had crept up to seventy or eighty yards away, and they were alongside in a matter of minutes. Already it was growing quite dark, with fog rolling in, blurring what little moon peeked through the cloudy night sky, but the flickery crimson glow climbing the horizon ahead of the tug provided sufficient, if eerie, light to see by. While Ferguson made the boat painter fast to a chain lashing, Ki jumped onto the scow with Laird right behind. Now it was Ki's turn to lead the way, across the slippery footing past mountainous piles of dead and dying salmon toward the turnbuckles at the bow.

"You're on to something, I know it," Laird growled. "What?"

Ki merely grunted enigmatically and concentrated on inspecting the thick braided cable that connected the scow to the tug. "Ah! Look here."

Laird peered, frowning. Strung unobtrusively in loops around the cable was what appeared to be a thin grayish ribbon, extending all the way from the tug to the turnbuckles, then stretching on to somewhere abaft in the scow.

"Che-rist!" Laird blurted. "That's double-tape fuse!"

"Uh-huh, and you know what that means," Ki said grimly. "It was sheer luck that I glimpsed the other end of the fuse dangling from the cable over on the tug."

"Wait here," Laird said and hastened back across to Ferguson. "There's a lantern in the boat," he told Ferguson. "Get it. I want to check—"

He didn't see Ferguson go into action, Laird swore later, after it was over and he'd had time to reflect. But he heard the half-stifled grunt as the seaman put his whole weight behind a lunging blow. He felt, too, a sheath knife rip through the heavy cloth of his peacoat and slice along the flesh of his rib cage. He was down then with the weight of the other on top of him, that was all he knew, trying to roll clear and get to his feet. It was no good. He twisted partway around and brought his elbow up in a short, vicious arc and smashed Ferguson's nose to a pulp as the sharp bone hit home.

Ferguson howled, but his knees still dug into Laird's back, and one of his strong hands locked into Laird's hair while the other poised again with the knife glinting

140

lethally in the dusky light. Laird jerked his chin instinctively into his chest, trying to protect his throat from the descending blade. Then suddenly, as surprisingly as the initial attack, there was a sodden smack of heavy flesh on bone, and Ferguson, his eyes abruptly gone blank and staring, collapsed atop Laird. The knife flew upward in a looping half circle and splashed into the water beyond the scow.

Somebody hooked fingers into Laird's collar and peeled him out from under Ferguson. Laird sat up. Ki stood there, legs spread wide and shoulders hunched. His fist was circled around the tail end of a thirty-pound salmon, his eyes fixed on a thin trickle of blood spreading outward from Ferguson's temple.

Laird staggered to his feet. "Thanks," he said and grinned. "I'm beholden to you twice now."

"Never mind that," Ki replied, tossing the fish aside. "First we'll take care of Ferguson. He won't stay out forever. Then we'll have a look at where the fuse runs."

They rolled Ferguson over; his nose was a red pulp and the scalp over his ear was laid open to the bone. Ki found himself thinking that a dead fish could pack one helluva solid wallop.

Between them they carried Ferguson to the dinghy and tied his hands and feet with marline and rolled him onto one of the thwarts. Laird refused to strip to the waist and let Ki tend his knife cut with gear from the first aid kit, obstinately insisting it was just a scratch that had already stopped bleeding. Ki figured to hell with him then and scrounged up the bull's-eye lantern from the lifesaving equipment.

They climbed back on the scow. The fuse didn't go very far back, they discovered, but it was buried under a mound of fish, which didn't help their dispositions any as they

141

dug down through the wet, heavy salmon. It was Laird who found the end of the fuse, where it threaded through a small hole in the lid of a canister. The canister was heavy and well protected against water, but his knife soon had the covering off. Inside the canister the fuse was crimped to a blasting cap; outside the label on the cannister read: HAZARD BRAND BLACK POWDER.

"There must be a quarter of a keg here!" Laird snapped. "Enough to blow this scow-load of fish to smithereens!"

"To sink it like a rock," Ki pointed out. "And to drag the tug down by the towline, if not rip off its stern and scuttle you that way."

"Yeah. All Ferguson would've had to do is light the fuse and row away. He'd have been safely ashore by the time the fuse burned to the canister, while we . . ." Laird clamped his jaw shut, seething. "History repeating itself, sort of. But there're a few loose ends. . . ."

After chucking the canister out into the water, they returned to the dinghy and rowed back to the tug. A rising breeze and mounting swell coming in made the going rough, especially, Ki observed, with Laird gritting his teeth from the sharp pain that had to be stabbing his rib cage. It was close to half an hour before they rounded in to the tug's rail.

The crew lifted Ferguson, who had regained consciousness by now, out of the dinghy and prodded him along behind Laird up to the boat deck quarters just abaft of the bridge. Despite their questions, neither Laird nor Ki offered any details, and Ferguson sagely kept silent. Reaching the room, Laird ordered the crewmen to disperse. Ki closed the door, staying close by it in case they got overly curious and tried to come in. Laird faced Ferguson, his mouth a tight, bloodless line.

"Now," he said, "let's start at the beginning. We found

the blasting powder. That's probably the way the *Hecate* broke up. It's just that nobody heard the explosion because of the wind and sea. Right?"

The tip of Ferguson's tongue passed across his lips. Otherwise they remained closed. Taking a quick step forward, Laird grabbed him by the shirtfront and slammed him against the bulkhead, backhanding him across the pale mouth. Ferguson slumped, groaning.

*"Right?"*

His furious shout and Ferguson's groanings masked any slight noise of the door easing slowly ajar behind Ki. Before Ki was aware of it, a gun muzzle appeared in the crack and jammed itself in his kidney, hard. It was a small caliber pistol, but it was big enough. The hand that held it belonged to one of the scow gang, one of the pair Ferguson had spoken to earlier. Hunch-shouldered, bull-chested, with a faced scarred by smallpox, the man wedged his way inside, still covering Ki. Showing a little ugly iron in his voice, he said, "Untie him, Cap."

Laird stiffened, his eyes shifting slowly to Ki. Ki let out his breath noisily. "It's a gun, Errol."

There was a moment of stillness, of malignant intensity.

Then, coldly furious, Laird untethered Ferguson and stepped back. In a wild rush, cursing, Ferguson swung both fists. The attack caught Laird flat-footed. He stopped one of the blows with his cheek, the flesh splitting over the bone. The second one landed under his ear, and he went down.

The gun muzzle in Ki's side jabbed him deeper, reminding him not to even think of interfering. Ki decided not to—not quite yet, anyway, and not out of fear; somehow he had a gut feeling there was more to this that needed playing out.

143

Dropping on his shoulder, Laird twisted aside, scrambling to get his feet under him again. He was on one knee when Ferguson's foot hooked into his body just under the ribs. He crumpled again, grunting from the stabbing pain above the point of his hip. Somehow he managed to roll, tangling Ferguson's feet as he aimed another kick. Maybe it was just that, or the rolling of the tug as she gathered way into the mounting swell, but Ferguson stumbled, fought for balance, and almost fell. It gave Laird time to weave to his feet. When Ferguson came in again, Laird was ready. He ducked a rounding left hand and hit Ferguson with a quick jab, then a countering right, putting everything he had behind it. It knocked Ferguson backward, and his head bounded off the mirror over the washbasin with a splintering crash. He didn't get up.

Laird drew deep sobbing breaths into his lungs, wincing at the pain where Ferguson's boot had landed. He shook his head, swiped absently at the blood welling down his cheek, and glared at the man holding the gun on Ki.

"Go on, shoot me. I'm the one you want, ain't it?"

The man behind Ki nodded. "I've been out to get you, okay. M'name is Shubert, same as my kid brother who served on the *Hecate*. He didn't come back. I was on the China run, a freighter, when I heard about it. It took me awhile to find you."

"Well, what's holding you back?"

"That's over. It wasn't your fault." Shubert lowered his pistol, then tucked it in his pocket. "I don't know how I know it, except there's something plenty screwy about this whole setup. I heard you talking a little just now. It looks like the same deal as the *Hecate*. It's a frame. You're to be the sack holder again."

"I know," Laird said. "Who's in this thing?"

"Can't say for sure." Shubert spat at the limp figure

144

of Ferguson. "The boxhead here, for one. The rest is a guess. They knew I was after you, so they figured me in for strongarm work, but they didn't tell me anything else." He glanced apologetically at Ki, then eyed Laird again. "What's next? You can count me for the home team, the scow gang, too. I'll see to that."

"Thanks," Laird said, then grinned at Ki. "I'm kind of overworking that word tonight, ain't I?"

Crossing to the washbasin, he cupped his hands under the cold water and splashed it over his face. Meanwhile, Ki looked over Ferguson. There were half a dozen cuts on his head, none appearing serious, and a a bruise coloring the underside of his jaw where Laird's blow had struck. When Laird was finished washing up, Ki took the basin of water and threw it in Ferguson's face. Ferguson came to sputtering and woozily sat up, shaking his head. Ferguson groaned as Laird pulled him to his feet and sat him on a chair propped against the bulkhead.

"Now," he began, but whatever else he was going to say was lost in the commotion outside as excited voices and bootsteps rapidly approached the room.

"Capt'n! Capt'n Errol!"

After a quick rap on the door, a number of crewmen squeezed into the room. Gimper Tynes seemed to act as their spokesman, blurting out, "Remember that fire we done been seein', Capt'n? Wal, we've come abreast of it now, and it positively ain't no tree fire. P'raps you should take a gander."

Keeping an eye on Ferguson, Laird and Ki peered out the window. By now the fire had burned low and was no longer a scarlet beacon enflaming the night sky. Its remaining fiery light, however, showed the source of the fire to be at the not-too-distant shoreline, partly on the bank and partly in the water. And by the skeletal shape of its still-blazing timbers and beams, the fire appeared to be consuming the remains of a boat—a boat about the size of a launch.

"Jessie!" Ki whispered.

Laird placed a hand on Ki's shoulder. "Easy, we don't know if that's the launch we sent to the cannery. It could be the other one, the one Vermillion's men escaped in, or it might be some other craft altogether." He turned to the crewmen, his voice taut and sharp. "Lower two dinghies. I want six volunteers, armed to the teeth just in case, but bring plenty of first-aid gear just in case of that, too. And I want it now, on the double!"

The crew rushed trampling back out.

The hand named Shubert remained behind, though, as did Ferguson. Laird dragged Ferguson out of the chair and said to Shubert, "You want to be counted in, eh? Well, there's a deck stores locker that oughta hold this rat, and it's going to be up to you to make sure he's there when we return."

Nodding, Shubert drew out his pistol and grabbed hold of Ferguson, shoving him out of the room, down the stairs. The deck stores locker on the main deck was open. Ferguson stumbled as Shubert nudged him over the weatherboard.

"Laird, you're crazy," Ferguson snapped.

"Yep," Laird agreed. "You gotta be to fish for a living. Move!"

Ferguson's eyes went from Laird to Shubert to the gun. His face was livid, and it looked for a moment as if he was going to make another break. He didn't. He snarled something and walked into the locker. Shubert dogged down the door and snapped the padlock, then handed Laird the key.

"Don't worry none, Cap. We's both be here when you get back."

146

Soon the dinghies were heading shoreward, Laird and Ki and two hands in one boat, the other four hands rowing the second. They found, when they landed, that the hulk of the once-blazing craft lay with her bow driven into the gravelly bank, a total ruin of fuming coals and embers.

There were no bodies around, nor sign of life. Ki checked for tracks but could not find any indication of anyone having come or gone. The only fact that seemed fairly certain was that the craft had been one of Vermillion's launches—but which one, at this point, was purely speculative. It appeared logical, however, to surmise that whatever had happened to the launch had happened out in the bay, and the launch had drifted in on the tide. The dead, if any, would have either sunk, floated ashore in other places, or been burned in the funeral pyre of the launch.

Ki thought of Jessie, fighting back fear for her, when a dark, shambling figure materialized in the shadowed timber. A creature that swayed as it slowly advanced, swinging and drooping its head grotesquely.

"A bear!" Quinotte barked. "Shoot him—"

"Wait!" Ki studied the swaying form. "That's not a bear!" He broke into a run, three of the crew trailing behind. Nearing the shadowy figure, he heard its pitiful whimpering cry, saw it collapse. It was a man, breathing raggedly, almost unconscious. A crewman made a quick return trip for a lantern, bringing Laird and the others back with him, and they all gathered around.

"It's Hoovis!" Laird said. "Grady Hoovis!"

The name sounded familiar to Ki, and he recognized him as one of the armed crewmen detailed to take the launch to the cannery—the launch that had carried Vermillion, his captured raiders, the Oceana wounded, and Jessie.

147

The half-comatose Hoovis was terribly beaten, bloody, and badly scratched by the underbrush through which he had fought his way. Cool water on his hurts and a stiff slug of whiskey brought him around a little, and from swollen and lacerated brows he cast a bewildered look around. He spotted Laird.

"Capt'n," he said weakly. "They ambushed us, them pirates . . . them's that'd getawayed in t'uther launch. Got us bad . . . sprung their own and torched our boat, left us for dead . . . all 'cept that lady. . . ."

"Miss Starbuck?" Ki prompted.

"Yeah . . . yeah, her. Ver-Vermillion took Miz Starbuck somewhere, I . . . I dunno . . ." Hoovis's ebbing strength failed him, and he lapsed into unconsciousness.

Ki fought panic as he tried to work out some solution to this newest disaster. At last, icy-faced, he told Laird, "Let's get Hoovis into a dinghy and shove off. There's nothing more here for us, but there's a certain gent aboard the tug I want a word with."

"You'n me both, Ki."

Leaving the charred, smoldering launch as they'd found it, Ki, Laird, and crew rowed out to the tug. Nobody spoke, and even the oars seemed strangely muffled. The loudest sound was the delirious moaning of Hoovis, the only survivor of the massacre other than Jessie—assuming Jessie was still alive.

Shubert was still standing guard at the deck store's locker, Ki was gratified to see when they finally reboarded the tug. As soon as Hoovis was out of the dinghy and being tended to, Laird went with Ki and opened the locker door.

Ferguson looked sick, either from fear, the cramped enclosement, or from twice being knocked senseless. Whichever, he sitting on an upturned bucket with another

148

one cradled between his knees. It held what remained of his supper. Trying to rise, he caught at the doorjamb as the tug rolled, pitched, and brought up with a sickening jerk on the towline. He swallowed something fighting upward in his throat.

Laird lit a cigarette and waited. So did Ki, wordless.

Ferguson said, "You're crazy. You—"

"We've been over that before," Laird said. "Are you going to talk?" He blew smoke into the narrow confines of the locker. Ferguson coughed and sank to his knees, moaning and clutching at the bucket. When he was through, he looked up at Laird. He didn't say anything.

Ki asked, "Where's Boone Vermillion?"

Ferguson shrugged. "You're no lawdog. You can't make me talk."

"That's where you're wrong," Laird said and stepped forward, his fists cocked. Ki stopped him with a hand on his arm, then smiled tight at Ferguson, his lips just crimping at the lower corners of his mouth.

"You're right-handed, aren't you?"

Ferguson nodded. "Why?"

"I know a few ways that encourage better than fists. Oriental ways. For instance, there's a nerve ganglion along the right side of your body, on account of you being right-handed, which's real easy to get at just under your armpit. That's a pressure point, y'see, and it can be painful." Ki spoke so casually, and so sincerely, that a visible chill went up the nape of Ferguson's neck. "It's not only the pain, of course. You might take the pain. No, it's that the nerve ganglion runs up from your groin, and if pressure is applied hard for very long, after that, well . . ."

"Well?" Ferguson swallowed thickly. "Well, what?"

"Well, you won't piss right. Always dribbling. And no more pleasuring the ladies afterward, either."

Ferguson looked horrified. "Y'mean I couldn't get it up?"

"Afraid so."

"I ain't heard tell of nothing so despicably low-down mean!" Ferguson was wild-eyed, a broken man. All vitality gone from his voice, he said, "All right. All right, Gawd, just hold off! Vermillion hired me. Me and Frenchie Tabac, to put the *Snohomish* down like the *Hecate*. Frenchie was to've crippled both engines, then I was to've opened the sea cocks to flood 'er."

"Tabac bungled that," Laird said.

"Uh-huh, so I laid low. One of Vermillion's men contacted me in Port Tenino, gave me the explosives to smuggle along, the idea bein' to rig 'em when it'd hurt you the worst. I figured it for tonight, what with your only tug and all them fish. But you was too smart for me."

"No, just simple. 'Simple Capt'n Errol.' That's what made it good. Sinking the *Snohomish* or this ol' bucket would've busted Oceana, and naturally, after the *Hecate* affair, nobody would've listened to my side. Me and my skipper's license would've been salted away for the next ten years. Providin', that is, I was still alive."

Again Ki demanded: "Where's Boone Vermillion?"

Ferguson shrugged. "Full-steamin' back to his own cannery operation, I reckon."

"That's a long run, even in a launch. You sure'n hell weren't going to row there in a dinghy," Ki said impatiently, urgently. "C'mon, where were you supposed to meet up?"

"Spyglass Crest. Vermillion's posted a couple of men up there to keep watch on your cannery."

"Yeah, it'd be a perfect vantage point," Laird allowed.

"Show me where it is on your chart," Ki told him, "and loan me a boat. Those guys are going to have a visitor tonight, but not the one they expect."

"You're insane, Ki! We'll chase out after Vermillion and—"

"In a tug dragging a scow of fish? We'd never catch up, and besides, we don't even know if he's aiming for his headquarters. One ambush has already been pulled on us, and he could well be around here somewhere readying another surprise, maybe even an attack on your cannery. But his lookouts might know, be able to at least give us a clue. In any event, they've got to be taken out."

"You may be on the right track, at that," Laird admitted. "You'll have plenty of help going along, too, my friend."

"I'm going alone. A boatload of armed men would be seen too easily, make too much noise, and'd send whoever's up there hunting for cover."

"But—"

"Your job is to get to the cannery, protect it in case of attack, and get all those salmon processed. You *must*, Errol! Think of the living, all those depending on you to pull Oceana through." Ki shook his head adamantly. "God willing, I'll find the lookouts and find out where Vermillion's heading and what's happened to Jessie. Whether I make it or not, you hightail for the cannery with barricades fixed and guns ready. Don't let Vermillion win by default! Don't argue, Errol. Get me on my way, pronto!"

★

# Chapter 12

According to Captain Laird's chart, Spyglass Crest formed a high, heavily wooded promontory overlooking the bay, situated near enough to the Oceana cannery to serve as a landmark for incoming craft. So basically all Ki had to do was row the dinghy in the same direction as the tug was heading, and he couldn't miss it.

That's all, just row there.

Row unceasingly hour after hour, straining rhythmically on the oars, hugging the shoreline to keep from being spotted. It was exhausting labor, and Ki put his mind into an almost trancelike state to endure the seemingly endless torture. Eventually, as the sky began graying with false dawn, he sighted the sheer, looming slope of Spyglass Crest. Nearing, he caught view of an inlet close by its rugged base, the narrow mouth dark with densely overgrown banks. There was no way for Ki to tell, without taking the channel, how far it went or if it would help him in tracking the lookouts posted somewhere up on the rise.

He was scanning the area, debating whether to follow the inlet, when above the dark land he glimpsed a curling wisp of smoke, like a sooty squirrel tail rising into the dim sky. A campfire? Noiselessly paddling to the beach, Ki ditched his boat in the underbrush and began snaking inland. Ears tuned for any unusual sound, eyes searching the rocks choked with wild timber and thorny growth, he gingerly crept toward the thread of smoke.

At last, cautiously parting a row of brush, Ki found he had reached the gravelly flood bank of the inlet, only a short ways from the bay. The smoke he'd spotted was not coming from any campfire. It was pluming from the thin funnel of a small, shallow-draft coastal packet, the craft not much larger than a private yacht. On the side of the funnel was painted a stylized mermaid.

"Vermillion!" Ki whispered to himself.

Sneaking up the inlet toward the packet, Ki breathlessly picked his way, gauging each footfall as though he were treading on eggs. He knew what his fate would be if anyone aboard saw and recognized him. And dawn was at hand. When at last he came abreast of the packet, he hunkered in the brush on the bank and paused to listen to the voices wafting clearly across the water.

"That fuckin' Ferguson must've loused up or chickened out," Boone Vermillion could be heard saying, although the man himself was out of Ki's range of vision. "We would've heard a blast by now if he'd done what I paid him to do. Why do I always get saddled with such peckerheads?"

There was a muttering of other voices—sounding vaguely like Jack Wing and Fantan Monger and a few other henchmen—all chorusing support for their boss.

Vermillion continued: "Well, it's up to us to stop Errol Laird now. We've got to wreck his tug and scow and kill every man jack, you understand. If they get word to the law of what we've done, we'll hang—all of us. If they don't, we're scott free and Oceana will be ruined, and I'll negotiate with the owner of record, that Starbuck bitch. Hell, she's only a woman; she'll sign over, no problem. Wait! There's the signal fire now, up on the crest! The tug is coming. Hurry, let's get to moving!"

Ki didn't wait. Easing into the water, he waded toward the packet, only his head showing above surface. A bell rang; steam hissed, and slowly at first, the packet nosed bayward down the inlet. Ki caught the gunwale and allowed himself to be towed alongside. Then, drawing himself aboard, he bellied down on the boiler deck while he took stock of the odds against him. Concentrated on the foredeck, their attention focused on the bay ahead, were the members of Vermillion's raider crew, each with a rifle glittering in the first pale flush of dawn. From the top deck above came Vermillion's bawled command for more speed as the packet reached the flaring mouth of the inlet.

Ki could not see Laird's approaching tug yet, but apparently Vermillion could from his vantage, for he shouted, "Yonder she comes, boys, headin' for the cannery. Good thing they don't know what's waiting for 'em!"

He laughed and some others joined him. "Jack, you and Fantan go below and bring Miss Rich-bitch up to the wheelhouse," he ordered. "I want her smack dab beside me while I'm pilotin' this job, just to show her who she's dealin' with. Now, we'll close with the tug at slow speed astern. And listen up for my orders, you understand?"

"Sure, boss. Whatever you want, you'll get."

Vermillion grunted and entered the wheelhouse, while Wing and Monger descended a ladder and disappeared through a doorway. A moment later they reappeared, forcing a protesting, fighting, scratching Jessie Starbuck back up the ladder to the top deck and into the wheel-house.

Eyes on the wheelhouse windows, Ki padded closer to the steps leading to the top deck, slipping into the gloom under the low main deck roof.

Behind him, a man's voice snapped, "Hold it, pal."

Ki pivoted—a tall, dripping figure hidden in the dark. An angular crewman with a sandy mustache was approaching, squinting to make out Ki's face, his revolver leveled. "I don't rec'lect you, buddy," he said with surly suspicion.

"I'm the agent for Mermaid Salmon." Ki spoke in a gruff, hoarse tone, taking a step toward the man. "What're you proposing to do?"

"Agent? Where'd you come from?" the man demanded. "How'd you get aboard?"

"Out of the bay," Ki replied, moving closer, wanting to take the man out quietly. "There's a long trail behind me."

Then some other crewman, who'd glanced their way, shouted: "Hey! There's that Ki bastard! Cut him down!"

Ki hit the deck, flinging *shuriken*. The man who'd questioned Ki was stung into action but doubled over with a steel disk in his chest before he could trigger. Another man came out of the shadows, grappled with Ki. Ki drove an elbow into the man's neck, slammed a fast one-two into the jaw. The man dropped like a weighted sack. But other men were converging.

Ki sprinted to the rail, put a palm on the worn wood, and lifted himself off the deck. His body vaulted into empty space, his dive carrying him in a deep, dizzy plunge into the chilly blackness of the bay. Water tore at his lungs. Pressure drummed at his ears. He kicked out his legs, clawed toward the surface. He came up into darkness and a confusion of shouting voices calling from the decks of the packet.

Guns were bellowing into the murky dawn, the gloom cut and laced by meshing streams of lead. Bullets angled into the water with a pelting splash that was like a light summer rain.

Ki was caught in the churning wake of the packet. A twist of current shot him down deeply, but he fought upward again to find the water stilled as the packet stopped. He swam toward it with powerful breast strokes, still a target for the guns lining its decks, and in desperation he decided to risk a wild ruse. After a volley of shots he cried out sharply as if in pain. He thrashed the water, then dived deeply.

"We got him!" shouted Vermillion exultantly.

More bullets sprayed the spot where Ki had been. Swimming underwater until he thought his lungs would burst, he broke clear, close in against the side of the packet. He caught a glimpse of Jack Wing, Fantan Monger, and some of the other raiders holding lanterns over the side, illuminating the water with an eerie, unreal brilliance. Then Ki went under again. When he surfaced he heard Wing mutter to someone else:

"He's done. He didn't come up."

"Maybe he's playin' possum," the man answered dubiously.

Jack Wing snorted. Ki held his breath and waited, sweeping his long hair out of his eyes. Gradually the lanterns were blown out. Ki paddled noiselessly along the side of the packet until his groping hand found a trailing rope end, and he held on to it while he heard Vermillion's voice yell for all hands to get back on deck.

A bell clanged in the engine room, and slowly the packet slid through the current again. With Vermillion at the wheel, Ki bet. Hanging on, he let himself be dragged through the mouth of the inlet, grateful at least that Vermillion, not knowing the channel, was proceeding at greatly reduced speed until he was out in the open bay. Otherwise he would have been drowned despite his efforts to stay afloat. He was also thankful that Vermillion was running his ship without lights, no doubt in the hope of drawing nearer to the tug before detection. The darkness that might work for the packet would surely work for him.

As soon as men's voices faded away above him, Ki braced himself, called upon his tiring muscles to lift himself in a hand-over-hand climb up the rope. He was winded and his arms were trembling when he reached the deck and climbed over the rail.

Ducking low behind a stack of crates—crates, he noticed, that were marked as containing ammunition—he took a moment to regain his breath and study the lay of the deck. He was one man against the entire bloodthirsty crew. Yet enough other crates, boxes, and barrels were piled about to provide him cover, and if he could avoid detection, there might still be a chance—a slim one, admittedly—of rescuing Jessie.

A crewman strode out of the shadows toward him. Ki, moving silently and with deadly intent, was upon the man before the latter could move to defend himself. Driving a shoulder into the man's chest, Ki stabbed a murderous, stiff-fingered blow to the man's heart, and the man collapsed without a sound. Letting the man slip to the deck, he padded aft, heart hammering beneath his ribs, nerves keened to detect the slightest warning sound.

Another man, dark-skinned, resembling a 'breed, suddenly materialized from around a corner. Ki paused, breathless, knife gripped in his hand. The man seemed to sense his presence, though, and pivoted aside, catching

158

a glimpse of Ki. Ki's left hand flashed out, caught the man's shoulder. In almost the same motion his knife hand snapped up and down; there was an ugly tearing sound as the blade sank into the man's chest. Blood spurted, splashing over Ki's fingers.

The crewman's escaping life was a faint moan on dark lips. Gripping him under the armpits, Ki hauled this body out of sight behind some barrels, then moved forward again, nerves screaming with tension. It seemed every board was alive with creaks. Yet with the raiding crew's attention turned bow-ward, he was able to squirm along the deck and up the ladder. Gaining the top deck, he crouched, his eyes on the wheelhouse. Figures moved in there, and Ki stalked them, alert for the first cry of alarm.

The cry was raised by a pug-ugly bruiser who sprang seemingly out of nowhere swinging a hatchet. The blade clipped down, slicing along the edge of Ki's arm, ripping open his sleeve and drawing blood. Then Ki was thrusting the blade of his own knife into the man's chest and wrenching upward. The man fell away, gushering blood and guts. Ki swerved, dropped another man coming up the ladder with a swiftly tossed throwing dagger, then leapt for the wheelhouse door just as three guns blazed in his face. Gunfire seemed to blow him away from the door and onto his back upon the texas deck.

Jack Wing and Fantan Monger piled headlong from the wheelhouse, leveling revolvers, swearing luridly. Monger spotted Ki first and fired wildly. Two bullets slammed into the deck planks inches from Ki's face, even as Ki, twisting frantically, loosened a *shuriken*. Monger cried weakly and lurched crumpling against Wing, upsetting Wing's aim. Ki hit him again with a second *shuriken*, and Monger, dropping his revolver, tottered tiptoe to the rail, over which he collapsed, as limp as a dishrag. From the wheelhouse came Vermillion's cursing while bells jangled furiously in the engine room. Then Vermillion, too, was shooting, blazing away through the open doorway.

Jack Wing, slamming against the wall of the wheelhouse to avoid being backshot by Vermillion, triggered swiftly at Ki. His bullet stung Ki's side as he rolled from the line of fire and came to his feet. Jessie was screaming from inside the wheelhouse, he heard, and Laird's tug was drawing close, too close to waste time. Daring fate, he charged Wing with drawn, bloody knife.

Wing fired point-black at his lunging figure. Ki waited for the shock of lead, but heard instead the hammer drop on an empty chamber. Wing flung his now useless weapon at Ki, who ducked, and they met in a savage, headlong rush. Wing's head butted Ki's jaw. Ki staggered, his teeth biting into his lip. Blood ran warmly in his mouth. Wing clawed for his skinning knife sheathed on his belt. Ki shifted, jumped in, then out again; in that brief interval, his knife sank hilt-deep into Wing's chest.

Below, tumult was breaking loose on the main deck, a chaos of confused men darting to vantage points from which they could see what was going on above. In the wheelhouse, Vermillion was slashing out the window glass, his pistol spraying bullets in a frantic effort to down Ki. The packet was lurching askew, veering from the open bay in an erratic curve toward the bank.

After hauling his knife from the body of Jack Wing, Ki flexed his weary muscles and vaulted for the wheelhouse again. Shadows of desperation and rage hollowed out the curved pockets under his blazing eyes. There was no caution in him, just a savage will to destroy.

To have barged in through the doorway would have been suicidal. Instead, while Vermillion was firing out one window, Ki dived through the broken-glassed window opposite. He had a swift glimpse of Jessie, loosely lashed to a chair, her face registering shocked surprise and hope. Then Vermillion was swiveling around, fear and loathing gnarling his features as he whipped his revolver around and triggered.

Ki threw himself to one side, the bullet meant for him knocking a chunk from a wheel spoke, then hit the floor as another slug sprayed dust and splinters into his eyes. Rolling to his knees, he heard a scraping, screeching sound and, glancing up, saw that Jessie had forced herself upright. Her clothes were torn and in disarray, but her eyes blazed fiercely. Dragging her chair and all toward Vermillion, she flung herself against his legs as Vermillion fired dead center at Ki.

The explosion rocked the small wheelhouse. Powder smoke drifted past Ki's straining eyes as he got his fingers around the handle of his knife. Vermillion fell to his knees but quickly regained his feet. His pistol roared. Ki saw the bright red muzzle-flash of gunpowder, felt the scouring slash of pain along his left shoulder.

Teeth bared in an angry grimace, he flicked his right arm back. He had to fight an overpowering dullness in his muscles, but his will made his injured muscles respond. At the end of the forward arc the knife left his shaking fingers. Speeding toward Vermillion, its death-stained blade caught him high in his chest. He dropped the pistol, both hands groping for the knife handle.

Ki staggered to his feet, only half conscious that Jessie had freed herself from the chair, though a strand of rope still dangled from one ankle. The deck was pitching, and Ki's legs were unsteady. Vermillion was still clawing at the knife, reeling drunkenly. Ki lunged at him, rammed his head against Vermillion's chin, drove a breath-wrenching

161

knuckler to the solar plexus, then watched the man collapse draped over the wheel.

Ki's own knees started to unhinge. He would have fallen, but slender arms were suddenly supporting him. "Like you said earlier, Jessie, it's nothing," he assured her, managing a tight grin.

There was shouting behind them. Boots thumped up the ladder and along the top deck toward the wheelhouse.

Jessie, slamming the wheelhouse door, fired the last couple of shots from Vermillion's pistol through the door to keep the converging men at bay. Ki nudged the body of Vermillion off the wheel and grabbed hold with one hand down which blood was slowly dripping. Jessie frantically rifled Vermillion's pockets for extra ammunition, reloading the pistol as fast as she could. Ki, meanwhile, rang for full speed ahead. And, surprisingly, got it.

The packet gathered headway swiftly. Ki spun the wheel, smiling grimly as wild yells greeted the sudden, unexpected swerving of the craft. Now they were steaming straight for the bank, and praying the engineer below would hold the throttle wide, Ki rang again for full speed.

Instead, the engineer answered the clamoring crew and cut steam. They were howling at him, obviously confusing him, but by the time he apparently caught the gist of their warnings, the packet struck the bank.

The terrific impact almost shattered the boat. It bent Ki double over the wheel and violently threw Jessie almost the length of the wheelhouse, and made the packet timbers shriek with strain. From below rose a profane chorus of yells, the hiss of steam, crash of furniture in the cabins, ripping the stanchions and supports, and the hollow impact of the stack falling, sheared off at the level of the texas deck.

Gathering breath into his lungs, Ki helped Jessie upright.

162

Then, exchanging a last worried look between them, they raced from the wheelhouse into what they feared would be a hail of deadly bullets. Instead, a frantic shouting echoed across the deck, blaring up at them:

"Hell's bells! The fire's kicked out from the boilers! Fire! Fire! Grab your buckets! If we don't get her out, the powder and ammo'll go higher'n a kite!"

Jessie relaxed with momentary satisfaction. Ki had done what he had come to do far more thoroughly than either could have hoped to dare. Already they could hear the crackle of flames and see a red glow building. Evidently, in preparation for battle with Laird, Vermillion had filled his packet like a floating arsenal, loaded with explosive matériel. And aware of the danger, his dazed and bewildered raiding crew were speeding to fight the fire, unwittingly leaving the stern unguarded. And there Jessie and Ki headed, hurdling the fallen stack, scrambling down ladders until they stood on the afterdeck, curtained now with smoke.

The dawn had become light now, the east rosy with the promise of the sun. Laird's tug, still towing the fish-laden scow, was bearing down on the packet, and they could see smoke and flame belching from her stubby funnel, her low, curling bow wave and the turbulence of the long wake stretching behind.

The one discordant note came as the tug's pilot—undoubtedly Errol Laird himself—wheeled the craft directly toward the stern of the doomed packet. Jessie and Ki had expected to swim ashore and ditch any pursuit in the thick woods. Failing that, they would have considered their work well done even though they lost their gamble for life. They were not afraid to die. Whatever fear they felt was for Errol Laird and his brave comrades, who were coming straight toward destruction. How could they warn them away before fire got to Vermillion's explosive cargo?

"Steer away!" Ki shouted as they gestured frantically with their arms. "Don't come near! Powder! She'll blow up, and—"

They gave up, realizing they couldn't be heard and their waving only seemed to be taken as signaling for rescue. But their yells had been heard by the fire-fighting packet crew. An angry voice roared behind them:

"Look aft, boys! There's that bitch and her squinty-eyed bodyguard! They done this! They shot up Vermillion and drove us ashore! Get 'em!"

Cursing savagely, quick to turn their fight against something offering a hope of victory, the cutthroat crew charged aft, shooting as they came. Lead whined about Jessie and Ki, threating to cut them down. Yet they hesitated to jump overboard until the tugboat was closer. Playing for time, Jessie leveled Vermillion's pistol, triggering six spaced shots at the forms avalanching from the smoke rift that hid the short. One man went down. The rest faltered, diving for cover.

Jessie hurled the empty gun at them contemptuously, then turned with Ki to dive into the bay. The pause had been enough. The prow of the tug was close now, and from above, Errol Laird was barking at them.

"Jump! Jump, you two, like you never jumped before!"

Ki went first, launching himself across that watery void with all the drive of his muscular thighs. Even so he would have missed the deck, save for the swelling bulge of the tug's hull bringing the gunwale closer. Jessie was not quite so lucky. Leaping, she caught the rail with a desperate reach, and her body fell, a dead weight against her arms. She smashed heavily against the hull, the impact almost tearing loose her hold. Then she was clinging there, numb-armed, with the bow wave tugging at her savagely, as if angry at losing her. Ki reached for her, and his strong hands pulled her over the rail.

The tug swerved away, heading for the open bay, the scow curving along behind. And looking back, Jessie and Ki saw the rush of men to the packet's afterdeck, their weapons leveling. From the decks of the tug came a deluge of covering gunfire, but surprisingly, not a muzzle flare winked from the Vermillion packet. The raiding crew, appearing to realize the hopelessness of it, gave up the fight and scrambled to save themselves, as smoke and flame obscured the scene.

The tug was hardly a half mile past when the packet blew up. The curtain of smoke with its edgings of flame was suddenly rent by a great geyser of timber and debris volcanoing skyward, then plummeting into the bay and along the bank as concussion reached the tug. For a flash Jessie feared the tug had been blown from the water, so terrific was the shock. The the tug settled and went on, the thump of her steam engine even and rhythmical.

At four knots, dragging the scow of fish, Laird piloted the tug toward his cannery. The jutting promontory of Spyglass Crest hid from the eyes of the Oceana crew the debris that had been Vermillion's packet, flotsam that would line the bank along miles of the bay.

★

# Chapter 13

Gathered comfortably in the warm office of Oceana Cannery, Jessie, Ki, and Errol Laird relaxed with brandy and coffee and gazed out of the large windows at the bay. The night overcast had parted for the moment, and a pale moon rode a starry sky, bathing water, forest, and rock with an eerie effulgence reflecting the peace in their hearts.

Ki sat somewhat more gingerly than the others. His wounds were cleaned, their flows of blood stemmed with thick salve and many windings of bandages. His right hand was stiff, and there was a shallow furrow gouged by a bullet that cut along the knuckles up to the wrist, but there was no indication that when healed, the wound would lessen his dexterity.

Jessie sat quietly, her face pensive as she stared at the moon-shimmery bay. Errol Laird, beside her, had one arm about her slender shoulders, his face pressed into the fragrant, wavy hair tumbling about her neck. From the large fish house behind them reverberated the noise of the cannery in operation. By craning slightly, they could have seen the scow parked under the cannery's long conveyor, and crewmen unloading the tons of salmon for processing. But they didn't bother, the sounds and smells coming through seeming music and perfume to Errol Laird—if not quite that to the others.

Thinking two's company, three's a crowd, Ki said when there was a lull in the conversation, "I think I'll cut myself a big slice of sleep."

"I think," Jessie agreed, "that's not a bad notion. Early tomorrow we'll have to be on our way to catch the first southbound steamer available. What're your plans, Errol? I mean, besides staying on for the season."

"Oh, I imagine one of the first things I'll be doing," Laird replied, "is to fire Foxclaw."

Jessie gasped. "Fire him?"

"Yep. Boot him out. Him and all the others who sided us. It's a cinch Vermillion would've run me out of the cannery business if it weren't for them. And I reckon it would be a fine thing if they started a little cannery of their own over on Half Moon River. If you could see your way clear to invest some Starbuck money to back it, and with Vermillion's fish ladder setup there, Half Moon River could develop a nice business in a few years."

"Consider the funds available," Jessie pledged, her eyes glowing. "Errol, you've figured out a way to show your men the Lairds never forget. You're just like your father."

"And yours, too, Jessie," Ki reminded her. "And you."

"Well, I try," Jessie demurred. "We always tried to take care of the deserving, because if we do, I guess they'll always take care of us."

Watch for

**LONE STAR AND THE
BLACK BANDANA GANG**

117th novel in the exciting LONE STAR series
from Jove

*Coming in May!*

America's new star of the classic western

# GILES TIPPETTE

author of *Hard Rock, Jailbreak* and *Crossfire*
is back with his newest, most exciting novel yet

## SIXKILLER

Springtime on the Half-Moon ranch has never been
so hard. On top of running the biggest spread in
Matagorda County, Justa Williams is about to become
a daddy. Which means he's got a lot more to fight for
when Sam Sixkiller comes to town. With his pack of
wild cutthroats slicing a swath of mayhem all the way
from Galveston, Sixkiller now has his ice-cold eyes
on Blessing—and word has it he intends to pick the
town clean.

Now, backed by men more skilled with branding irons
than rifles, the Williams clan must fight to defend
their dream—with their wits, their courage, and their
guns. . . .

Turn the page for an exciting preview of

SIXKILLER
by Giles Tippette

Coming in May from
Jove Books!

It was late afternoon when I got on my horse and rode the half mile from the house I'd built for Nora, my wife, up to the big ranch house my father and my two younger brothers still occupied. I had good news, the kind of news that does a body good, and I had taken the short run pretty fast. The two-year-old bay colt I'd been riding lately was kind of surprised when I hit him with the spurs, but he'd been lazing around the little horse trap behind my house and was grateful for the chance to stretch his legs and impress me with his speed. So we made it over the rolling plains of our ranch, the Half-Moon, in mighty good time.

I pulled up just at the front door of the big house, dropped the reins to the ground so that the colt would stand, and then made my way up on the big wooden porch, the rowels of my spurs making a *ching-ching* sound as I walked. I opened the big front door and let myself into the hall that led back to the main parts of the house.

I was Justa Williams and I was boss of all thirty-thousand deeded acres of the place. I had been so since it had come my duty on the weakening of our father, Howard, through two unforunate incidents. The first had been the early demise of our mother, which had taken it out of Howard. That had been when he'd sort of started preparing me to take over the load. I'd been a hard sixteen or a soft seventeen at the time. The next level had jumped up when he'd got nicked in the lungs by a stray bullet. After that I'd had the job of boss. The place was run with my two younger brothers, Ben and Norris.

It had been a hard job but having Howard around had made the job easier. Now I had some good news for him and I meant him to take it so. So when I went clumping back toward his bedroom that was just off the office I went to yelling, "Howard! Howard!"

He'd been lying back on his daybed, and he got up at my approach and come out leaning on his cane. He said, "What the thunder!"

I said, "Old man, sit down."

I went over and poured us out a good three fingers of whiskey. I didn't even bother to water his as I was supposed to do because my news was so big. He looked on with a good deal of pleasure as I poured out the drink. He wasn't even supposed to drink whiskey, but he'd put up such a fuss that the doctor had finally given in and allowed him one well-watered whiskey a day. But Howard claimed he never could count very well and that sometimes he got mixed up and that one drink turned into four. But, hell, I couldn't blame him. Sitting around all day like he was forced to was enough to make anybody crave a drink even if it was just for something to do.

But now he seen he was going to get the straight stuff and he got a mighty big gleam in his eye. He took the glass when I handed it to him and said, "What's the occasion? Tryin' to kill me off?"

"Hell no," I said. "But a man can't make a proper toast with watered whiskey."

"That's a fact." he said. "Now what the thunder are we toasting?"

I clinked my glass with his. I said, "If all goes well you are going to be a grandfather."

"Lord A'mighty!" he said.

We said, "Luck" as was our custom and then knocked them back.

Then he set his glass down and said, "Well, I'll just be damned." He got a satisfied look on his face that I didn't reckon was all due to the whiskey. He said, "Been long enough in coming."

I said, "Hell, the way you keep me busy with this ranch's business I'm surprised I've had the time."

"Pshaw!" he said.

We stood there, kind of enjoying the moment, and then I nodded at the whiskey bottle and said, "You keep on sneaking drinks, you ain't likely to be around for the occasion."

He reared up and said, "Here now! When did I raise you to talk like that?"

I gave him a small smile and said, "Somewhere along the line." Then I set my glass down and said, "Howard, I've got to get to work. I just reckoned you'd want the news."

He said, "Guess it will be a boy?"

I gave him a sarcastic look. I said, "Sure, Howard, and I've gone into the gypsy business."

Then I turned out of the house and went to looking for our foreman, Harley. It was early spring in the year of 1848 and we were coming into a swift calf crop after an unusually mild winter. We were about to have calves dropping all over the place, and with the quality of our crossbred beef, we couldn't afford to lose a one.

On the way across the ranch yard my youngest brother, Ben, came riding up. He was on a little prancing chestnut that wouldn't stay still while he was trying to talk to me. I knew he was schooling the little filly, but I said, a little impatiently, "Ben, either ride on off and talk to me later or make that damn horse stand. I can't catch but every other word."

Ben said, mildly, "Hell, don't get agitated. I just wanted to give you a piece of news you might be interested in."

I said, "All right, what is this piece of news?"

"One of the hands drifting the Shorthorn herd got sent back to the barn to pick up some stuff for Harley. He said he seen Lew Vara heading this way."

I was standing up near his horse. The animal had been worked pretty hard, and you could take the horse smell right up your nose off him. I said, "Well, okay. So the sheriff is coming. What you reckon we ought to do, get him a cake baked?"

He give me one of his sardonic looks. Ben and I were so much alike it was awful to contemplate. Only difference between us was that I was a good deal wiser and less hotheaded and he was an even size smaller than me. He said, "I reckon he'd rather have whiskey."

I said, "I got some news for you but I ain't going to tell you now."

"What is it?"

I wasn't about to tell him he might be an uncle under such circumstances. I gave his horse a whack on the rump and said, as he went off, "Tell you this evening after work. Now get, and tell Ray Hays I want to see him later on."

He rode off, and I walked back to the ranch house thinking about Lew Vara. Lew, outside of my family, was about the best friend I'd ever had. We'd started off, however, in a kind of peculiar way to make friends. Some eight or nine years past Lew and I had had about the worst fistfight I'd ever been in. It occurred at Crook's Saloon and Cafe in Blessing, the closest town to our ranch, about seven miles away, of which we owned a good part. The fight took nearly a half an hour, and we both did our dead level best to beat the other to death. I won the fight, but unfairly. Lew had had me down on the saloon floor and was in the process of finishing me off when my groping hand found a beer mug. I smashed him over the head with it in a last-ditch effort to keep my own head on my shoulders. It sent Lew to the infirmary for quite a long stay; I'd fractured his skull. When he was partially recovered Lew sent word to me that as soon as he was able, he was coming to kill me.

But it never happened. When he was free from medical care Lew took off for the Oklahoma Territory, and I didn't hear another word from him for four years. Next time I saw him he came into that very same saloon. I was sitting at a back table when I saw him come through the door. I eased my right leg forward so as to clear my revolver for a quick draw from the holster. But Lew just came up, stuck out his hand in a friendly gesture, and said he wanted to let bygones be bygones. He offered to buy me a drink, but I had a bottle on the table so I just told him to get himself a glass and take advantage of my hospitality.

Which he did.

After that Lew became a friend of the family and was important in helping the Williams family in about three confrontations where his gun and his savvy did a good deal to turn the tide in our favor. After that we ran him

177

against the incumbent sheriff who we'd come to dislike and no longer trust. Lew had been reluctant at first, but I'd told him that money couldn't buy poverty but it could damn well buy the sheriff's job in Matagorda County. As a result he got elected, and so far as I was concerned, he did an outstanding job of keeping the peace in his territory.

Which wasn't saying a great deal because most of the trouble he had to deal with, outside of helping us, was the occasional Saturday night drunk and the odd Main Street dogfight.

So I walked back to the main ranch house wondering what he wanted. But I also knew that if it was in my power to give, Lew could have it.

I was standing on the porch about five minutes later when he came riding up. I said, "You want to come inside or talk outside?"

He swung off his horse. He said, "Let's get inside."

"You want coffee?"

"I could stand it."

"This going to be serious?"

"Is to me."

"All right."

I led him through the house to the dining room, where we generally, as a family, sat around and talked things out. I said, looking at Lew, "Get started on it."

He wouldn't face me. "Wait until the coffee comes. We can talk then."

About then Buttercup came staggering in with a couple of cups of coffee. It didn't much make any difference about what time of day or night it was, Buttercup might or might not be staggering. He was an old hand of our father's who'd helped to develop the Half-Moon. In his day he'd been about the best horse breaker around, but time and tumbles had taken their toll. But Howard wasn't a man to forget past loyalties so he'd kept Buttercup on as a cook. His real name was Butterfield, but me and my brothers had called him Buttercup, a name he clearly despised, for as long as I could remember. He was easily the best shot with a long-range rifle I'd ever seen. He had an old .50-caliber Sharps buffalo rifle, and even with his old eyes and seemingly unsteady hands he was deadly anywhere up to five hundred yards. On more than one occasion I'd had the benefit of that seemingly ageless ability. Now he set the coffee down for us and give all the indications of making himself at home. I said, "Buttercup, go on back out in the kitchen. This is a private conversation."

I sat. I picked up my coffee cup and blew on it and then took a sip. I said, "Let me have it, Lew."

He looked plain miserable. He said, "Justa, you and your family have done me a world of good. So has the town and the county. I used to be the trash of the alley and y'all helped bring me back from nothing." He looked away. He said, "That's why this is so damn hard."

"What's so damned hard?"

But instead of answering straight out he said, "They is going to be people that don't understand. That's why I want you to have the straight of it."

I said, with a little heat, "Goddammit, Lew, if you don't tell me what's going on I'm going to stretch you out over that kitchen stove in yonder."

He'd been looking away, but now he brought his gaze back to me and said, "I've got to resign, Justa. As sheriff. And not only that, I got to quit this part of the country."

Thoughts of his past life in the Oklahoma Territory flashed through my mind, when he'd been thought an outlaw and later proved innocent. I thought maybe that

179

old business had come up again and he was going to have to flee for his life and his freedom. I said as much.

He give me a look and then made a short bark that I reckoned he took for a laugh. He said, "Naw, you got it about as backwards as can be. It's got to do with my days in the Oklahoma Territory all right, but it ain't the law. Pretty much the opposite of it. It's the outlaw part that's coming to plague me."

It took some doing, but I finally got the whole story out of him. It seemed that the old gang he'd fallen in with in Oklahoma had got wind of his being the sheriff of Matagorda County. They thought that Lew was still the same young hellion and that they had them a bird nest on the ground, what with him being sheriff and all. They'd sent word that they'd be in town in a few days and they figured to "pick the place clean." And they expected Lew's help.

"How'd you get word?"

Lew said, "Right now they are raising hell in Galveston, but they sent the first robin of spring down to let me know to get the welcome mat rolled out. Some kid about eighteen or nineteen. Thinks he's tough."

"Where's he?"

Lew jerked his head in the general direction of Blessing. "I throwed him in jail."

I said, "You got me confused. How is you quitting going to help the situation? Looks like with no law it would be even worse."

He said, "If I ain't here maybe they won't come. I plan to send the robin back with the message I ain't the sheriff and ain't even in the country. Besides, there's plenty of good men in the county for the job that won't attract the riffraff I seem to have done." He looked down at his coffee as if he was ashamed.

180

I didn't know what to say for a minute. This didn't sound like the Lew Vara I knew. I understood he wasn't afraid and I understood he thought he was doing what he thought was the best for everyone concerned, but I didn't think he was thinking too straight. I said, "Lew, how many of them is there?"

He said, tiredly, "About eighteen all told. Counting the robin in the jail. But they be a bunch of rough hombres. This town ain't equipped to handle such. Not without a whole lot of folks gettin' hurt. And I won't have that. I figured on an argument from you, Justa, but I ain't going to make no battlefield out of this town. I know this bunch. Or kinds like them." Then he raised his head and give me a hard look. "So I don't want no argument out of you. I come out to tell you what was what because I care about what you might think of me. Don't make me no mind about nobody else but I wanted you to know."

I got up. I said, "Finish your coffee. I got to ride over to my house. I'll be back inside of half an hour. Then we'll go into town and look into this matter."

He said, "Dammit, Justa, I done told you I—"

"Yeah, I know what you told me. I also know it ain't really what you want to do. Now we ain't going to argue and I ain't going to try to tell you what to do, but I am going to ask you to let us look into the situation a little before you light a shuck and go tearing out of here. Now, will you wait until I ride over to the house and tell Nora I'm going into town?"

He looked uncomfortable, but, after a moment, he nodded. "All right," he said. "But it ain't going to change my mind none."

I said, "Just go in and visit with Howard until I get back. He don't get much company and even as sorry as you are you're better than nothing."

181

That at least did make him smile a bit. He sipped at his coffee, and I took out the back door to where my horse was waiting.

Nora met me at the front door when I came into the house. She said, "Well, how did the soon-to-be grandpa take it?"

I said, "Howard? Like to have knocked the heels off his boots. I give him a straight shot of whiskey in celebration. He's so damned tickled I don't reckon he's settled down yet."

"What about the others?"

I said, kind of cautiously, "Well, wasn't nobody else around. Ben's out with the herd and Norris is in Blessing. Naturally Buttercup is drunk."

Meanwhile I was kind of edging my way back toward our bedroom. She followed me. I was at the point of strapping on my gunbelt when she came into the room. She said, "Why are you putting on that gun?"

It was my sidegun, a .42/40-caliber Colts revolver that I'd been carrying for several years. I had two of them, one that I wore and one that I carried in my saddlebags. The gun was a .40-caliber chambered weapon on a .42-caliber frame. The heavier frame gave it a nice feel in the hand with very little barrel deflection, and the .40-caliber slug was big enough to stop any thing you could hit solid. It had been good luck for me and the best proof of that was that I was alive.

I said, kind of looking away from her, "Well, I've got to go into town."

"Why do you need your gun to go into town?"

I said, "Hell, Nora, I never go into town without a gun. You know that."

"What are you going into town for?"

I said, "Norris has got some papers for me to sign."

"I thought Norris was already in town. What does he need you to sign anything for?"

I kind of blew up. I said, "Dammit, Nora, what is with all these questions? I've got business. Ain't that good enough for you?"

She give me a cool look. "Yes," she said. "I don't mess in your business. It's only when you try and lie to me. Justa, you are the worst liar in the world."

"All right," I said. "All right. Lew Vara has got some trouble. Nothing serious. I'm going to give him a hand. God knows he's helped us out enough." I could hear her maid, Juanita, banging around in the kitchen. I said, "Look, why don't you get Juanita to hitch up the buggy and you and her go up to the big house and fix us a supper. I'll be back before dark and we'll all eat together and celebrate. What about that?"

She looked at me for a long moment. I could see her thinking about all the possibilities. Finally she said, "Are you going to run a risk on the day I've told you you're going to be a father?"

"Hell no!" I said. "What do you think? I'm going in to use a little influence for Lew's sake. I ain't going to be running any risks."

She made a little motion with her hand. "Then why the gun?"

"Hell, Nora, I don't even ride out into the pasture without a gun. Will you quit plaguing me?"

It took a second, but then her smooth, young face calmed down. She said, "I'm sorry, honey. Go and help Lew if you can. Juanita and I will go up to the big house and I'll personally see to supper. You better be back."

I give her a good, loving kiss and then made my adieus, left the house, and mounted my horse and rode off.

183

But I rode off with a little guilt nagging at me. I swear, it is hell on a man to answer all the tugs he gets on his sleeve. He gets pulled first one way and then the other. A man damn near needs to be made out of India rubber to handle all of them. No, I wasn't riding into no danger that March day, but if we didn't do something about it, it wouldn't be long before I would be.

A special offer for people who enjoy reading the best Westerns published today.

# WESTERNS!

## NO OBLIGATION

### Mail the coupon below

To start your subscription and receive 2 FREE WESTERNS, fill out the coupon below and mail it today. We'll send your first shipment which includes 2 FREE BOOKS as soon as we receive it.

# From the Creators of Longarm!

LONE★STAR

Featuring the beautiful Jessica Starbuck
and her loyal half-American half-
Japanese martial arts sidekick Ki.